A Dangerous Occasion of Sin

Sheila Storey

First published in paperback 2019 by Sheila Storey Publishing

Copyright © Sheila Storey 2019

All rights reserved

ISBN 9781706466659

A Dangerous Occasion of Sin

Chapter 1

1958

Saint Ambrose Roman Catholic Church rose out of Sebastopol Terrace like a fortress. It was almost the size of a cathedral but had neither the grace nor the splendour. Too bricky, thought Rita Fellowes as she walked towards the church with her brother Tim Forrester.

"Too many bricks, that's the problem", said Rita.

"What? What's too many bricks? What are you talking about?" asked Tim.

"That church. It's just got too many bricks. It's ugly," she replied.

"But a church that big needs a lot of bricks," laughed Tim and gave her a quizzical look.

Rita stopped walking and faced her brother.

"You could have stopped this Catholic nonsense years ago, Tim. It's ridiculous bringing up your daughter to be a Catholic when you're not one yourself. First the Baptism, then Confession and Communion and now this Confirmation."

"I knew this had nothing to do with bricks", replied Tim. "I know you don't like coming here, Rita, and I'm glad of your support all the more for it. But you know I promised Agnes just before she died that I would bring Judy up as a Catholic and I will not break that promise. You know that."

"Now, Tim, I know this might sound harsh but your wife isn't here anymore and can't decide how you and Judy should live your lives. When a person dies they can't expect those who go on living to live in the particular way that they have chosen for them. The living must go on living their own lives."

"Rita, that's enough. You know I won't break that promise. Anyway, when Judy's grown up she can choose for herself whether she wants to be a Catholic or not."

"You're joking, Tim! Too late! Give me a child before he's seven and he's mine for life. That's the Jesuits for you."

"I think that was Aristotle."

"I don't care *who* said it – it's true!" Rita snorted.

They'd continued walking and entered the gloom of Saint Ambrose, Rita tall and slim with an air of confidence, Tim shorter and broader but with the same brown hair and hazel eyes. They settled down on a hard bench near the front and Rita looked around. Pictures of the fourteen Stations of the Cross were hung at intervals on the two side walls, one of the many statues showed Christ's bleeding heart and a huge crucifix hung over the altar.

"There's nothing but pain, sorrow and punishment in here." Rita muttered.

Tim gave her a warning look and she resigned herself to watching her niece's Confirmation ceremony.

Meanwhile relatives and friends of the children to be confirmed were filtering down the aisles. Across from Rita and Tim sat Sandra and Joe Conti. They were notable for their attractive but completely opposite appearance. Sandra was petite with shoulder- length blond hair and eyes of oceanic blue which could either lure you in or leave you cold. Joe was tall and broad with his black hair betraying his distant Italian ancestry. His dark brown eyes would never leave you feeling cold. Sandra nudged Joe,

"That's Rita Fellowes over there in the grey suit and blue hat. She's not a Catholic. I wonder what she's doing here."

Joe had no idea who Rita Fellowes was and had no inclination to find out or to be told.

"She's the one who's always in "County Life" magazine", continued Sandra. "She's on lots of committees, married to Edward Fellowes, the solicitor. Lots of power locally."

Joe had long since lost interest in Sandra's social ambitions, what she called "status in the community". He couldn't understand her restlessness. Was she bored? Was she bored with him? The one saving grace in their marriage, thought Tim sadly, was their only child, David, doted on by both of them.

Joe's eyes wandered and he gazed at the statue of Saint Joseph, his namesake. He mused on the tradition in his family. For generations, even before they had settled in England from Italy, the eldest son had always become a priest. They grew up knowing that this was their destiny just as a prince knows he'll become king. He thought of the family chalice which was handed over to the next newly ordained Conti at his Ordination. He also knew that that chalice had been a poisoned one for his brother, Patrick. Joe was convinced that deep down but hidden from his own view, Patrick had not wanted to be a priest and had certainly not been a suitable candidate for such a position. Now, Sandra was working on David to follow the family tradition. He was the next generation of the Conti family and she was determined to see the family chalice presented to him.

Sandra glanced at Rita Fellowes again. She must somehow make herself known to her at the Confirmation breakfast after the ceremony. Her mind wandered. She hoped Judy, the scruffy little tomboy whom their son David called his best friend, would not be there. She recalled how strange it had been on David's first day at school when this "creature", as Sandra called her, and David had latched onto each other and had never been apart since. She was a scruffy, unkempt child, not at all a suitable friend for

David and anyway she was a girl! Surely at their age boys played with boys and girls played with girls. This was unnatural. Of course, Joe wasn't bothered. He said the girl was polite and clearly intelligent and it didn't really matter if she was scruffy, as Sandra called it. The girl lived at the bottom of Sebastopol Terrace and that said it all, thought Sandra. She didn't want her hanging round David at the reception and showing them up.

Organ music was playing a gentle background to the whispering and ponderings of the congregation and Joe mused again on his marriage. Sandra had been the prettiest, most vibrant girl at the Tennis Club where he and his friends used to meet regularly. She was the most popular girl, all the boys vying for her attention. Joe thought about his brother Patrick again. Patrick had been told by their mother from the day he was born that he was going to follow the family tradition of the eldest son becoming a priest. So at five Patrick had said that he wanted to be a priest; at ten he said that he knew he was going to be a priest. By his teenage years he was calling it his vocation. Patrick was good-looking, athletic and sociable. He seemed to enjoy being attractive to girls and Joe knew that Patrick had been out with girls, even Sandra. Joe was astonished when Sandra suddenly turned her attention from Patrick to Joe himself. He knew he looked like Patrick but he didn't have his flair or charisma. But she utterly captivated Joe, lured him into the ocean and in the blur of a whirlwind they were married. Looking back now, twelve years on, with the organ music flowing sweetly, he wondered how on earth it had happened. But, David, their lovely son made it worth it or so Joe thought.

Across the aisle, the music was also having an effect on Tim Forrester sitting beside his sister, Rita, when he should have been sitting there with his wife, Agnes. The music drifting through the church had reminded him of Agnes' funeral. Judy was only three when Agnes died. Both families had been against the marriage – Tim's because he was marrying a Catholic and Agnes' because she wasn't marrying a Catholic. But where was love in all this? Tim thought. Isn't Religion about love? Both families called themselves Christians. It sometimes seemed to him that Christianity had become a religion of separation, not love. Tim shook his head.

Rita glanced at her brother. She, too, pondered on her life as she sat on the hard bench and succumbed to the gloom of the church. She and her husband Edward - or Ted as she called him - had never had children but had never missed them either. She had a busy life with her charitable causes, fund raising, and Ted's business and social life. She imagined that people would have expected her to take on the mother's role when her sister-in-law died but she could not pretend to have maternal feelings. She did what she had time for here and there and Tim managed very well. In fact, she told herself, supporting him in this church was way beyond the call of duty.

The organ music suddenly changed volume and tempo and the bishop in his regalia walked on to the altar with the priest and altar boys. The whispering and shuffling stopped as, in boy and girl pairs, the children walked forwards to the altar from the back of the church. Sandra knew that David and "the creature" would have paired up. She would be in some hand-me-down dress with her long lank hair unwashed as usual. She didn't want Rita Fellowes to see her connected in any way to the Sebastopol scruffs. She turned and strained to watch the children walking up the aisle and spotted David. Relief! No sign of "the creature".

After the ceremony the congregation moved into the Parish Hall where the Confirmation breakfast had been laid out. Sandra was working out how to inveigle herself into Rita Fellowes' company. A girl had now joined Rita and the man Rita had been sitting with. Sandra knew that he wasn't Rita's husband because Sandra had seen their photos in "County Life". The girl who'd joined them had glossy hair and a little veil held in place by a circlet of flowers. She wore a ballerina length white organdie dress short enough to show gleaming white leather pumps. She was exactly the kind of girl that Sandra expected the Ritas of this world would be related to. David Conti rushed up to his parents and they congratulated him on his Confirmation.

"The next ceremony will be your Ordination and the presentation of the family chalice!" Sandra gushed.

"Sandra!" warned Joe. "Not now!"

They couldn't have their regular argument here in public but he would not let history repeat itself.

"Mum, Dad, come over here."

Sandra was astonished to find David leading her directly towards Rita Fellowes.

"Mum, Dad, this is Judy's Dad and Auntie Rita."

Sandra stared at the girl. She was "the creature"; a clean, feminine, pretty version of "the creature".

The synchronicity of "the creature" being Rita Fellowes' niece struck Sandra dumb and she stood staring at the girl who was now Judy, never to be "the creature" again. For the first time that day, despite having been in a church for nearly two hours, Sandra Conti spoke to God – "Thank you", she said. She recovered sufficiently to shake hands with Rita and Tim and say to Judy,

"My goodness, you look lovely, Judy."

Rita laughed,

"Ha! You wouldn't say that if you saw her as she usually is. Oh, but of course, you will have seen her because she's David's best friend. I bet you didn't recognise her."

Sandra was astonished at Rita's *laissez faire* attitude to Judy's appearance when she herself was so well groomed.

"Yes, Judy comes over to play so we see her quite often."

Tim Forrester smiled,

"Yes, and it's always a pleasure to see David over at our house too. I'm glad we live so close and they can pop in and out. I wouldn't have the time to take Judy round to friends' houses if they weren't nearby."

Sandra was shocked to hear that Tim thought that Sebastopol Terrace was near to where she lived. She didn't want Rita to think that she was in any way connected to Sebastopol Terrace, the dirty end of town. However, in reality there was only a hill between them. Go up the hill to the church from Sandra's house and down the hill on the other side is Sebastopol Terrace. The church stood at the top as the barrier between the two. Tim continued.

"It's odd how we've never all met before considering how long Judy and David have been friends."

Sandra continued smiling. She knew exactly why they'd never met. She didn't mix with folk from that end of town. But of course that would have to change now. But Rita provided a reason why they'd never met.

"It's probably because we're not Catholics; otherwise we'd have seen each other at Church. Nora Wilson, Tim's neighbour, used to take Judy to church but she's old enough to go on her own now."

"It's Judy's birthday next Saturday", Tim said. "We're having a little party - just David and a few friends from school. Oh, you'll know of course because we've already given out the invitations."

Sandra remembered the invitation and had decided that "unfortunately" they would be doing something else on that day and David wouldn't be able to go. How things can change in an instant.

"Oh, yes, thank you. We've got the invitation but I just had to check on something before we could reply. But, yes, as it turns out David is free next Saturday after all so he will be able to come."

Tim laughed.

"It wouldn't be much of a party for Judy if David wasn't there! Come over at the end of the party and have a cup of tea and some birthday cake."

"How lovely!" Sandra enthused and, how very useful, she thought. Rita Fellowes was bound to be at her niece's party. If she played her cards right she might be about to enter the higher echelons of the small town's high society.

Chapter 2

During the following week Sandra and Joe's regular argument blew up yet again. Joe heard Sandra talking to David about his calling to be a priest.

"Sandra, it's not a calling if you've been told from day one that you're going to be a priest. He must have a choice. He must be able to discern a true vocation from the expectations of other people."

"But it's your own family's tradition. Don't you want your own son to be a priest?"

"Only if he truly wants to be. It has to come from within him himself. If he wants to talk about it, that's fine. But *you* bring up the subject yourself every single day. He's only eleven years old for heaven's sake. He's got his whole life in front of him."

Joe knew that the highest accolade for a Catholic mother was for her son to be a priest. He remembered that after his brother Patrick's ordination his parents had been the first people to receive the blessing from the newly ordained priest. They'd knelt at the altar rail before their son and after the blessing his mother hugged Patrick, weeping uncontrollably. She spoke of a priest being Jesus' representative on earth. She would say that when a priest enters your house it is Jesus coming in. For your own child to have the calling to do this was the highest possible blessing. Joe thought about their parish priest, Father O'Brien, who would come round to the family house and drink their whisky, talk about horse racing and say nothing in the least uplifting. Joe couldn't remember Jesus doing that. He smirked at the thought of how different the New Testament would be if what his mother thought was true. Father O'Brien would be invited to dinner from time to time. His mother would use the special china, the prized wedding present from years back and rarely used. The wine was poured into fine glasses and Father O'Brien didn't hold back. No trace of Jesus there, Joe used to think. How could his mother not see this? Why did she constantly remind Patrick that he was going to be a priest? Did she fear that his potential vocation would fade? If that happened how would she fill the huge void that would open up in her life? Would she then have to turn her attention to Joe himself and start trying to mould him into the shape of a priest? He was adamant that history would not repeat itself with David.

He turned to Sandra.

"I don't want the same thing to happen to David as happened to Patrick."

Sandra flinched.

"What do you mean?"

"Well, you should know. You were Patrick's girlfriend for a while, weren't you? A man with so many girl friends and such an interest in his own looks is hardly priest material. He was sucked into the family tradition without him even knowing it."

"Patrick wasn't my boyfriend. We went out together as friends. He told me he liked female company so I was happy to be his friend because he was interesting and lively and it suited me to be with him. I knew he was going to be priest so why would I think he was my boyfriend?"

Joe was taken aback. He'd been convinced that Sandra and Patrick had been going out together as boyfriend and girlfriend but it appears that Patrick had been honest about his intentions.

However, the truth was that Sandra would never tell Joe what had really happened. She and Patrick had indeed been romantically attached and she certainly hadn't known that he was going to be a priest. She'd decided that although he was a bit unreliable and flirtatious he was definitely the one for her. He would settle down once they were married. But, one day when she was at the Conti family home and Patrick had gone upstairs to find a book that he was going to lend to her, Mrs. Conti came into the room and gently closed the door.

"You do know that Patrick is destined for the priesthood, don't you, my dear? I imagine he has already told you because his vocation is so strong that he talks about it constantly. He can't be swayed so it would be unfortunate if you were to become, er, how shall I put it, too fond of him. You're an attractive young woman. You'll soon find another young man."

There was a vase of lilies on the piano. Mrs. Conti lifted them out and pushed them, dripping wet into Sandra's arms.

"I'm sure you're a good girl. You understand. Perhaps it would be better if you didn't see Patrick again."

No, Sandra did not understand. She was so shocked that when Patrick suddenly came back into the room she rushed past him, tears streaming down her face.

"Mum, what on earth's going on?"

"She seemed a bit upset, didn't she? Have you got the papers you needed to show Father O'Brien? He's expecting you. He wants you to help him with a bit of parish work as well. It'll get you acquainted with some of the work you'll be doing when you're a priest yourself."

Mrs. Conti smiled her cosy, smug smile.

"Do you know, Patrick, that Father O'Brien reminded me just the other day of the time when you were about five and you burst into the sacristy and said, "Father, I want to be a priest!" Do you remember what he said to you?"

"Yes. He said that if you know that you want to be a priest then that is exactly what you will be because it is written on your heart and on your soul."

Sandra had heard this conversation because she had waited in the hall to recover herself before she left the house. It was at that moment that Joe had come down the stairs. He saw that she was upset, standing in the hall with tears on her cheeks and water from the lilies slowly dripping down her dress. He didn't ask her what the matter was but simply asked if he could help and tenderly walked her home. The transition from Patrick to Joe had been that simple.

Up until that point Sandra had ignored Patrick's brother but now she turned the spotlight fully onto him. She decided that he was actually better marriage material than Patrick. Joe was stable, more serious than his flighty brother and although not quite as good-looking he did resemble Patrick to a certain extent. So Sandra kept accidentally bumping into him, asking him questions, giving him compliments. Joe was used to being in the shadow of his loud, popular brother and couldn't understand Sandra's sudden interest in him. Anyway, wasn't she Patrick's girlfriend? Joe didn't want to step on Patrick's toes but it seemed that Patrick was already going out with another girl. Although Joe was confused he didn't waste time thinking about it as he had already drowned in those eyes. At the end of the summer holidays Patrick started at the seminary and Joe and Sandra went on to eventually get married.

*

The week after the Confirmation ceremony passed by in a cool atmosphere until the day of David's birthday party arrived. The mood lightened and Sandra stood in front of the wardrobe wondering what to wear.

"Honestly, Sandra, you'd think we were going to the Queen's Garden Party. It's just the aftermath of a kid's birthday party. We'll have a cup of tea, make polite conversation and be on our way. What's the big deal?"

But he knew what the big deal was. It was Sandra's hopes of entering what she considered to be the local High Society. She was hoping that Rita would be there. Joe reckoned that if that's what it took to make Sandra happier and satisfied then perhaps their life together might improve. Joe took David into the garden to kick a ball around until Sandra called David in to get ready for the party. Joe smiled at the thought of the scrubbing and polishing that David would have to go through in order to be presentable to the blessed Rita. Finally, they were ready and Joe delivered David to the party. Sandra and Joe spent the next two hours at home with their own thoughts. At last it was time for them to set off to number 2 Sebastopol Terrace. Sandra had to admit to herself that she'd never actually been to the bottom end of Sebastopol – she only knew it through reputation from when she was a child. Her only association with it was Saint Ambrose church at the top of the hill. The entrance to the church was on her side of the hill so she'd had neither need nor desire to venture around the church to the other side of the hill.

*

This area at the back of the church was known locally as "the Crimea". It was a grid of streets named after the battles of the Crimean War and was a mixture of Victorian terraced cottages and large two-storey semi-detached houses. It had in recent years, unbeknownst to Sandra, lost its scruffy reputation and become very popular with Estate Agents. It was now known as an area of bijou artisan cottages and spacious Victorian villas with extensive gardens. Sandra was astonished as she and Joe walked down the tree-lined terrace past the well kept cottages. The little park on the left, Alma Park, where David and Judy often played, had borders bursting with cottage garden flowers. A pink rose bush rambled over the silver filigree gate. Sandra felt that she'd entered a different world, far removed from her orderly post-war semi on the new estate on the other side of the church. She allowed herself a brief moment of shame when she remembered how she'd recoiled when "the creature" had told her where she lived. How could she have got it so wrong? They arrived at the Forrester's just as the last party-goers were leaving.

"Come in, come in!" Tim called. "Good to see you again."

They walked straight into the living room off the street and gaped at the floor to ceiling bookshelves along one wall, the deep settee, piled with cushions and the Moroccan lamp casting a warm glow in the corner. Sandra wondered if this was what was meant by "bohemian". Then she caught sight of Rita's willowy, erect figure through the window as they walked through the kitchen into the long, narrow garden. Rita was as elegantly and perfectly groomed as she had been at the Confirmation and Sandra wondered why she didn't help in the choice of Judy's clothes. She had obviously chosen Judy's Confirmation outfit. They walked towards the little group of garden chairs and Tim introduced Edward, Rita's husband.

"You've already met Rita, my sister, and this is Edward, Rita's husband, my brother-in-law.

Sandra and Joe were warmly welcomed by Rita and Edward and Tim went to prepare the tea. David and Judy ran up to say hello and soon wandered off. In the living room David picked up one of Judy's birthday cards showing a huge guardian angel with a hand on each shoulder of a little boy and girl as they crossed a rickety bridge.

"This is from your Auntie Marie, the nun, isn't it? The picture looks like you and me but she doesn't even know us. It must be odd not knowing your own auntie, although I suppose she isn't your real auntie, is she?

"No, I don't even know if I have any aunties. I think of Dad as my real Dad but I know he isn't. My real parents are just like ghosts in the background. No-one knows who they were. I was only a baby when I was adopted."

Rita looked over at them.

"They're never short of something to do. They just look after themselves for hours."

Joe was surprised but delighted when Sandra became the girl from the Tennis Club again. She complimented Tim on his lovely house and garden, her pretty face lighting up with enthusiasm, her newly returned vibrancy enveloping them all as they chatted easily through the remains of the afternoon. It had been a beautiful day and now it was the luminous time – the late afternoon of a sunny day when a glow illuminates the earth. The flowers wafted in the warm air as the group relaxed into the softness. No shadow crossed the sweet lawn that afternoon.

Joe Conti warmed to Edward, Rita's husband. He was a tall, well-made man, a good ten years older than Joe. He was calm and quiet with an air of detachment but by no means unsociable. He turned to Joe,

"I gather you play chess, Joe. Tim's been teaching Judy to play chess for a long time now and when I saw her playing with David I asked him who'd taught him and he said that his Dad was teaching him. Tim and I sometimes play but it's difficult for us to play regularly. So, I'm getting out of practice and wondered whether you'd like to have a few games sometime?"

"I certainly would. I don't play regularly anymore so I'm out of practice too."

"Well, how about this Friday evening? Come over to us and bring Sandra too. We're in Regent Square, number 8; it's just between George Terrace and Hannover Street."

Sandra was well aware of where Regent Square was and who lived there. No need for directions. It was a square of white Georgian houses with black wrought iron balconies. Wisteria floated along from balcony to balcony in the spring. A little copse stood in the centre of the square surrounded by railings to be used only by the residents. It was Sandra's dream. But, as Joe explained, Sandra wouldn't be able to join them next Friday because there was no-one to look after David and it would be too late for him to be left alone. Joe asked Sandra,

"Would you mind if I played chess with Edward on Friday evening because it means that you'd have to stay at home with David?"

He looked at Edward and Rita,

"You see, our usual babysitter's away."

Sandra answered graciously that of course he should go. He hadn't had a chess partner for a while and it was a good opportunity to get back into the game. But her disappointment was palpable. Not only would she have had the opportunity of seeing if she could join any of Rita's groups but she would have stepped into a house in Regent Square. She could only guess what it would look like inside but her imagination furnished the house with antiques, rich velvet drapes and exquisite good taste. Mulling over her disappointment, her thoughts were suddenly interrupted by Rita suggesting that in that case Sandra should come over for coffee on the Friday morning while David was at school. Rita had been thinking that Sandra's youth and vitality might liven up one of her charity foundations and she now had the perfect opportunity to investigate the possibility. She didn't know whether Sandra would be interested or not. If only she knew. The dreams of one meet the needs of another. So as the earth continued its journey around the sun the little group sat together in the warm softness of the early evening, each happy with their own thoughts. All was well.

*

Tim Forrester had lived in Sebastopol Terrace since his marriage. It had been Agnes and her sister Marie's family home and the two girls had continued living there after both parents had died relatively young, one not long after the other. This seems to happen when there is a deep connection between married couples or so well-wishers kept telling them, as if that piece of information would somehow reduce the shock of losing both parents. Agnes was working as a secretary while Marie was still at school and it was at the engineering works where she worked that Agnes met Tim. Because Tim wasn't a Catholic he'd had to take instruction in the Catholic faith and decide whether to convert before being allowed to marry. He'd privately objected to being ordered about by a group of people to whom he had no affinity, people who gave themselves the power to decide whether he could marry or not, but he took the instruction, nevertheless, in order to marry Agnes. Needless to say, he did not convert. Agnes wanted Tim to live in her house in Sebastopol Terrace after they were married and insisted that Marie should live with them. This was not how Tim had wanted to start his married life but he could see that it was the only way. Although Tim's refusal to convert did not prevent the marriage, Tim had to promise that any children born as the result of their marriage should be brought up in the Catholic faith. That didn't worry him. They would cross that bridge when or if they came to it. In fact, that bridge never even came into view and they decided to adopt a child. That child was Judy.

It was at about this time that Marie suddenly announced that she was to become a nun, but not a teaching or a nursing nun. She was going to enter an enclosed order where she would contemplate and pray for the rest of her life. The arguments against this, which were many and varied from both Agnes and Tim, were ignored and Marie disappeared from their lives. It was only three years later that Agnes died. Nora Wilson, the Forrester's next door neighbour offered to look after the three year old Judy while Tim went to work. A few years later, Nora's son and his wife who lived just round the corner in one of the villas in Inkerman Terrace had a little boy, Billy, and Nora willingly took him in every day too. Nora's life was full now and the sorrow she'd suffered from losing her husband in the war lessened. So after the shocks and sadnesses that had befallen the Terrace, life settled down while the inhabitants re-arranged their lives and yet again, the need of one person was fulfilled by the matching needs of another.

For Sandra, the week following the little tea party at the Forrester's passed in a flurry of excitement, turning into anxiety and agitation by Thursday. What should she wear when she went to Rita's for coffee? What was the etiquette for this kind of occasion? Would she somehow let herself down? She needn't have worried. Rita's need for someone with Sandra's energy and flair to join her charitable organisation was met by Sandra's eagerness to be part of Rita's life. Sandra came away from the splendours of Regent Square so happy and amazed that it had all been so easy. As she strolled home it occurred to her that "the creature", that unkempt child who David had latched onto and who Sandra had kept at arm's length was the cause of her not only meeting the famous Rita Fellowes but working with her. If she'd had her way and managed to prise David out of Judy's clutches this would never have happened. How strange.

Joe was relieved to hear that all had gone well and he looked forward to a quiet evening with Ted in that same house in Regent Square.

Chapter 3

On a cold, wintry day in February, David and Judy walked by the stream that flowed from the old part of town into the woodlands. It was their favourite walk and they watched it change through the seasons. David was quiet and Judy knew that he was still mourning for his favourite football team. Most of the Manchester United team had been killed in a plane crash and David had been wrestling with his feelings over this.

"I went to see Father O'Brien about it. I asked him why God had allowed it to happen."

Judy waited. Then David said that she just wouldn't believe what Father O'Brien had said.

"He said how dare I question Almighty God. Who did I think I was to suggest that God, the maker of Heaven and earth, could do something *wrong* just because I couldn't understand it. Honestly, Judy, he went mad. He said that I should ask for absolution immediately because if I went through that door and got run over I would go straight to Hell. He said that if I still wanted to be a priest I would have to repent my sin of pride."

"So what did you do? Did you ask him to hear your confession, like he said?"

"I didn't think I'd done anything wrong but I had to. I didn't bother explaining to him that I hadn't been offending God, that I just really wanted the answer. He would have just gone mad again so I said my confession."

"What penance did he give you?"

"He said I had to say the Rosary."

"Have you done it yet?"

"No, I think you should only say the Rosary because you want to. It shouldn't be a punishment. It's like at school when they give you a poem to learn because you've done something wrong. That's not what poems are for. Just think if you were a poet and you found out that your poems were being used as a punishment. Well, it's the same thing."

They walked on into the woods. Then David said,

"So when I went home I asked Dad why God had let the team be killed. I didn't tell him about the carry-on with Father O'Brien."

"Did your Dad go mad as well?"

"No, Dad's not like that. He said that God gave us free will so it was the pilot's decision to try to take off in bad weather. If we didn't have free will we'd just be puppets. But he said, as well, that we can ask God for His help and then He *will* intervene. So, he said that if the pilot had asked God for his help in making the decision whether to take off or not then God would have guided him because he'd asked Him to."

Judy thought for a minute.

"So what we could do now is ask God to *always* help us and guide us and then we'll *always* make the right decisions."

David stopped walking.

"That's brilliant. Let's do it now."

They knelt down on the wet grass and made up a prayer that they knew would keep them safe forever, believing that God would guide them always to make the right decision. Little did they know how important that little prayer was to become. They walked on, following the stream to where it joins the river. The naked trees were black, stark against the backdrop of hills and a few raindrops fell. They sat in the shelter of an old barn that was gradually falling down but still offered refuge. They called it "their barn" as they'd sheltered there so many times. David pulled at the grass that had started growing through the floor. He looked forlorn as he twisted the grass into little knots.

"There's something else." David said. "I heard Mum and Dad arguing about me again last night. I'd got up to go to the toilet and they didn't know I could hear but I've heard this argument loads of times. It was that row again about me going straight to the seminary or going to school here first and then on to the seminary afterwards. Mum wants me to go straight to the seminary instead of to Saint Francis School here. She said that it's like school at first and then when you get to eighteen you decide whether to stay on and train to be a priest or leave. Dad wants me to go to school here first and he said that I should even go on to University or do some work before deciding for definite whether I really want to be a priest because once a priest always a priest. I heard him say that you have to make huge sacrifices when you become a priest and you should at least know what these sacrifices are before you make them. Then he said that odd thing again about not wanting history to repeat itself."

Judy leaned against the back of the barn.

"But what do *you* want to do?"

"I really want to go to school here first – the seminary's miles away. But then I feel guilty as if I'm putting off my vocation because I really do want to be a priest. I've wanted to be a priest for as long as I can remember.

*

Edward and Joe's chess games were now an established part of their week. They were well matched and enjoyed the companionable silence of those evenings. But one evening Joe seemed out of sorts and unusually lost three games in a row. Edward sat back.

"You're not your usual self tonight, Joe. Anything wrong?"

"Oh, I'm sorry, Edward, but yes, I do have something on my mind."

Joe went on to tell him about the ongoing argument with Sandra about when David should start at the seminary.

"Well, I'm on your side, Joe. Much better to be sure about something that will change your life forever. Yes, he is much too young."

"I wonder if Sandra has mentioned this to Rita", Joe said. "She looks up to Rita, I know that, and she'd listen to her."

Edward laughed.

"Well, if she has I know what the answer will be. As you know, Joe, we're not Catholics and Rita is – how shall I put it? – actually anti-Catholic. It all goes back to when Tim's wife Agnes died. She made him promise that he would bring Judy up a Catholic even though the rest of the family were not Catholic apart from Agnes' sister, Marie. But, she'd joined an enclosed order of nuns at a very young age. I think Tim felt let down that she didn't come and help with Judy when Agnes died. But the order's very strict and Tim and Judy rarely hear from her. So sad."

Edward shook his head.

"But to get back to David's situation - if Sandra has asked Rita's advice – I know what the answer will be!"

Sandra had, in fact, told Rita about her dilemma and Rita had tactfully but clearly explained that she thought that Joe was right. Sandra had reluctantly let go of her insistence that David should go straight to the seminary and hugely surprised Joe one evening with the news that David could go to Saint Francis, the local secondary school. Joe silently rejoiced and wondered how this had happened. He suspected Rita's involvement. All was well again.

The dank, grey days of February gave way to March as we always rely on them to do. April came in surprisingly sweet and warm as David and Judy walked to the bandstand in Alma Park. They had little Billy Wilson with them to give Nora, his grandmother, time to do her spring cleaning. They had always called him "little Billy" although he was getting quite big now.

"They've decided." David said. "Dad and I won. I can go to school here!"

They grabbed hands and ran round the bandstand. Out of breath and laughing they sank to their knees. Billy ran squealing after them and David lifted him high into the air and whirled him round.

"That's the best news." Judy gasped.

David was to go to Saint Francis, the boys' Catholic school and Judy had already been accepted at Saint Catherine's Convent school. The schools were only one street away from each other and the priests and nuns spent too much energy trying to keep the boys and girls apart.

Sandra hadn't been pleased with Joe's insistence that David shouldn't go to the seminary yet. She knew that she would have missed David horribly if he'd gone away but that was all part of the sacrifice made by a priest, she thought. The family makes the sacrifice too but for huge rewards. She hugged to herself the thought of her son being a priest; being the person who people come to in times of trouble but in times of joy too; the man looked up to in the community; a man above the normal run of life, detached, inviolate.

She'd taken Rita's advice and given in. Although part of her still rankled, there was a huge new delight in Sandra's life which went some way to taking her mind off her obsession with David's future. Her work with Rita Fellowes had taken off just as she'd hoped. Rita, for her part, was very pleased with how things had turned out. She'd been right about Sandra's energy bringing new enthusiasm into the group. She'd had some clever ideas for fund raising; ideas which attracted a younger group into the functions. Sandra was now on the committee among the "County Life" set. She was astonished at how quickly it had all happened and all because of David's little friend. She was slightly ashamed that she'd called Judy "the creature" and had assumed that she had a rough background. On the other hand, thought Sandra, if a child looks unkempt and wild that's exactly what people will think. But Rita Fellowes was her aunt! Sandra grinned to herself. You just never know, do you?

"What are you grinning about?" Joe asked.

Sandra hadn't heard him come in. He didn't like the way they'd been arguing so much recently and he made up his mind to try to make things better between them. He put his arms round her and said how pleased he was that she was looking happy. He wanted her to be happy, he said. She smiled up at him. He guessed what would please her:

"Tell me about your work with Rita. We haven't had time to talk properly for ages. How's it going? Are you enjoying it?"

Joe had hit the right note and Sandra described her fund-raising ideas with all her old enthusiasm, her eyes lighting up to their most intense aqua blue. Joe drowned in them once more.

*

"Mum and Dad have stopped arguing at long last." David told Judy as they sat in the bandstand again later in the week.

"Is it because the decision about school's been sorted?"

"I think there's more to it than that. Mum's doing a lot of work for your Auntie Rita and I think she's really enjoying it. It gives her something to do anyway. It must be really boring just being at home all day."

"I know. I'm going to go to work when I'm grown up. I heard Auntie Rita telling Dad that your Mum was doing a lot of good work for her Charity and how glad she was that she'd met her. And Dad's been playing chess with your Uncle Ted nearly every week. Isn't it funny how they all got together after they'd met at the Confirmation?"

"I'm glad. You and me – we've been friends for years and our families didn't even know each other. I think that's odd. How did that happen?"

"I don't think your Mum liked me. I don't know why. She's all right now, though. Maybe it was because she didn't know Dad or Auntie Rita and Uncle Ted. Perhaps now she knows them and likes them she thinks it's ok for us to be friends. When I was at your house once I heard your Mum say to your Dad that she couldn't understand why you were always with me and that boys of your age usually go round with other boys."

"What did Dad say to that?"

"He said that when we went to secondary school we'd probably make other friends and just naturally drift apart."

"No chance of that", said David, "blood brothers for life."

"Blood sisters, you mean." Insisted Judy.

"Blood cousins? Asked David.

"That's the one." Laughed Judy.

Chapter 4

Judy met David as usual to walk to school together but this time she was bursting with news.

"You know the old lido that's been boarded up for years – the building they used as a storehouse during the war and then just left boarded up again?" Judy asked. "We've never seen it because they closed it before we were even born. Well, guess what! Uncle Ted said that it's going to be restored and it's going to open in time for the summer holidays!"

David gaped. "Really? Honestly?"

A whole summer of swimming and playing around in an open-air swimming pool opened up before them. They walked over to the old building at the side of the park that they passed every day, forgetting what it had been and only seeing it for the eye-sore that it had become. They tried to see through the fence but it was well boarded and they couldn't see if work had even started on it.

"I hope it's not just one of those rumours." Sighed David.

"No. Uncle Ted knows people on the Council and he said they're going to announce it next week."

Judy went on to tell David that Uncle Ted had told her all about the lido. That the lido, along with Alma Park and the bandstand had been built in 1858 by a local industrialist called Sir William Alexander. He'd said that this was to give some refreshment to his workers, who mostly lived on the then new estate, which was now nick-named "the Crimea", and was where Judy and Tim actually lived. He'd added that there were pictures of the lido in books on the town in the library but the pool had been closed for so long that most people had either never heard of it or had forgotten about it. They arrived at the playground just as the bell went. They made their way straight to the classroom with the possibility of a lido swishing around in their minds for the rest of the day, taking precedence over nouns and verbs, multiplication and the Ten Commandments.

On the Monday following Judy's news there was a report in the local paper detailing the refurbishment of "the magnificent Victorian lido on the edge of Alma Park in Sebastopol Terrace", showing pictures of it in its heyday. The town's engineers and surveyors had been exploring the possibility of reopening the lido and had come to the conclusion that it was viable. Work had already started and it should be ready to open in time for the summer. The report continued that the local technical college, art college and museum were all involved and that the work was already slightly ahead of schedule.

As the few remaining months went by, local businesses and organisations saw the opportunity of getting their names involved in the enterprise and donated money towards the many extras that would be needed. Everyone wanted a piece of the lido. The Coronation parties had raised the spirits of the town a few years earlier and now the lido would enliven them once again.

The early April sunshine had been a false hope. The showers soon arrived and caught David and Judy as they were walking towards the stream from the bandstand. They ran to the old barn to wait for the burst of sunshine which would mark the end of the torrent.

"Have you noticed the fairy tale names that football teams have?" Judy asked.

"Fairy Tales?"

"Yes, they have names like Rangers and Rovers, Wolves, and Wanderers. There's even a Crystal Palace. There's a Forest and Hearts. There are loads of them. Haven't you ever noticed? While we're waiting for the rain to stop let's make up stories but we have to use the names of football teams."

David frowned. The rain was still very heavy and they'd already played "I Spy" in the barn so many times that there was nothing left to spy.

"Well, ok but you go first."

Judy smiled and thought for a few minutes. She looked up and said right, she'd got one:

"The Rangers and Rovers were out and about with their Wolves last night. The Wanderers were lurking in the Forest but Hotspur was on watch. They'd raided the Arsenal, and guns were leaning against the trees. I asked them who they were looking for and they said Alexandra Crewe and Stanley Accrington. I didn't tell them but I knew that Alexandra and Stanley were safe in the Crystal Palace in the Queens Park. The End."

David pretended to be annoyed.

"Hey, you did that a bit quick, didn't you? You've done it before, haven't you?"

Every Saturday night at six o'clock Tim listened to the football results to check his Football Pools and Judy would lie on the settee sewing a tapestry of stories around the magical names of the football teams.

"Yes, I listen to the football results and the stories come into my head."

"You've never told me that before."

"I know you like football so I thought you'd think it was daft."

"You're never daft, Judy. You're dead clever."

Then Judy remembered something important that she'd meant to tell him.

"I read an article in a magazine about something that we do. I thought we were the only ones who do it but other people do it too and it's even got a name."

"What is it? What do you mean?" David asked.

"You know when we know what each other's thinking and when we can sort of send messages to each other but without actually saying it and sometimes at night as we're dropping off to sleep we find out in the morning that you were thinking the same thing as me or I was thinking the same thing as you? It's called "Telepathy". The magazine described how to do it but we already do it."

David thought it over.

"It's a power, isn't it? Or is it a gift? I wonder if we were born with it or if it grows? Perhaps it works if you've got this telepathy thing and then you meet another person who's got it. Perhaps that's why we're friends because we've both got it but of course we didn't know at the time. It's sort of going on behind the scenes."

The shower had stopped as quickly as it had begun and the sun shone on the raindrops and pattered off the trees as they walked on to the river.

"I'll miss you when you're a priest. I can't imagine not knowing you and not being with you all the time but I suppose that's why telepathy is going to be useful."

"What do you mean you'll miss me? Are you going away? Couldn't you live in the same place? You could be a teacher or something in the same town."

"But we wouldn't be able to be friends. Priests aren't allowed to have friends who are women."

"I know priests can't get married but having friends is different."

"I don't think they see it like that. It would be what Father O'Brien would call "a dangerous occasion of sin."

This troubled David. He had never seriously looked into the finer points of being a priest. He thought of being a priest purely from the description his mother was always giving – a representative of Jesus on earth. He'd been an altar boy for years and loved the solemnity, the ritual, of the mass and the mystery of how the priest has the power to change the bread and wine into the body and blood of Christ. When he passed the wine to the priest to be consecrated, he felt that he was part of the process himself, almost a priest. In a few years time he would have those Godly powers himself. He thrilled at the thought. Anyway, he thought, to get back to Judy's point, Jesus had friends who were women so it must be ok.

While the Conti family were eating their evening meal, David brought up the women friend question.

"Is it true that priests can't have friends who are women?"

Sandra replied first,

"Priests dedicate their lives to their duties and their parishioners so they don't have time for personal friends."

"So they can't have friends who are men either? It's not just women?" David asked.

Joe knew from his brother Patrick's experience that it *was* all about women. Patrick had been told at the seminary that they should discourage visits from females, including even their own mothers and sisters. He'd told Joe, laughing, that when they went into the local town they had to go in threes. Apparently, the temptations of the town would be too much for a trainee priest on his own but even more tempting if two like-minded seminarians were let loose together. Three was a safe number, especially if one of them was from a higher year. So Joe answered David's question:

"Actually, it *is* all to do with women. You could have male friends who are also priests or you could be the friend of a family, like when Father O'Brien comes here and came to our house when I was a child, not just on a Parish call but to eat with us sometimes. The church thinks that because priests mustn't marry, it's better that they should keep away from women or they might be tempted."

"So does that mean that I can't be Judy's friend anymore when I'm a priest?"

Sandra spoke quickly,

"All your friends will be other priests, David, and you'll have lots of fun. It's not all deadly serious. Do you remember when Father O'Brien told us how he has holidays with his old friends who were at the same seminary and what a good time they all have?"

Joe couldn't imagine a worse holiday than being with Father O'Brien and a gang of his friends. He pulled a face,

"Well, I hope he goes to places where there's enough whisky for them all."

"Joe, there's nothing wrong with a priest having alcohol. After all, Jesus turned water into wine."

"Jesus had wine because their water wasn't much good and there wasn't a lot of it around either. The wine in the Bible wasn't like the strong wine we have now and certainly not the strength of spirits like whisky."

And so the argument continued until David wished he hadn't asked the question. He'd have to ask someone else but certainly not Father O'Brien whom Joe had just called a raging alcoholic causing Sandra to be horrified that Joe should so horribly criticise "Jesus' representative on earth".

"I've told you before, Sandra. Father O'Brien and some other priests that I could mention do not represent the Jesus that I know. I don't think Jesus would be very pleased at the thought of these people claiming to represent him."

Sandra fell silent and they finished their meal in quiet unease.

*

On their way to school David told Judy that his parents were arguing again and that their arguments were always about the church or priests.

"It's a bit like Auntie Rita and Dad", Judy responded. "Auntie Rita's always telling Dad that I don't need to be a Catholic. She says he doesn't have to follow what my mother wanted. But he says he promised so he must."

"Yes", David agreed. "Your Dad's right. We must keep promises. I've promised God that I'll be His priest so I must keep that promise."

"Doesn't a promise have to have two sides to it?" Judy asked.

"What do you mean?"

"A promise is when two people agree to something or one person asks for something and the other person agrees. Well, how do you know that God's accepted your promise? What if God actually wants you to do something else? Your promise to be a priest is only on your side. You don't know if God's accepted it."

David said nothing. He hadn't thought of that. Judy often came up with ideas that took him by surprise. Where did she get them from? Judy sensed David's unease and added hurriedly,

"That doesn't mean that you don't want to be a priest. But perhaps you can just choose for yourself. Perhaps God doesn't call people to be a priest – He just lets them choose for themselves."

David remembered Joe telling him about God giving us free will. There might be no such thing as a vocation. He ruminated on this in silence as they walked on and came to the school yard. They were just in time, as the bell was ringing and they hurried into their classroom, sat at their adjoining desks and turned their attention to the first lesson which was, as usual, Religious Studies. They were doing a revision of the whole of the catechism ready for their end of term test which was conducted by priests from the nearest seminary. David had a thought. He would put Judy's theory to the priest.

Chapter 5

It was July and the boards and sheeting that for decades had hidden the old lido from view were due to be removed very soon. David and Judy still couldn't see anything. They'd searched for gaps in the barriers but it was all wrapped up like a huge birthday present. They were crossing the park one Saturday on their way to Judy's Auntie Rita's when they stopped dead in their tracks. The gates to the lido had been unwrapped. It was the most beautiful sight they had ever seen. The blue painted ironwork rose into an arch. Dolphins' tails enfolded mermaids, crescent moons looked down on ripples and starfish danced on the crests of waves. A man was standing beside them and said in an awed voice,

"Just look at the craftsmanship of that gate. You wouldn't find anything like that these days."

"How did they make them?" asked a stunned David.

"They heat the iron and then mould it while it's soft. But they weren't just blacksmiths; they were artists. It takes your breath away."

Judy realised at that moment that she wanted to create beauty – that was to be her vocation. She had chosen it herself.

"I'm going to be a blacksmith." She announced.

"But you can't be a blacksmith. I don't think girls are allowed to do that." David said.

"Why not? What's being a girl got to do with it?"

"I don't know."

"And, what's more", added Judy, "why can't girls be priests?"

"That's because Jesus was a man."

"But he had lots of women in his group when he was here. He chose a woman to be the first person who saw him when he came back from the dead. So why can't women be priests?"

"I don't know."

David decided that there were too many things that he didn't know. He would ask the Religious Studies examiner that question too. He thought that Judy would make a good priest and they could have been priests together. His thoughts rambled on in his troubled mind. But they turned their attention back to the gates and traced the figures with their fingers. They wondered who had made them, what their names were, where had they lived? Through the gates they could make out two long arcades in the same graceful blue ironwork down each side of a passageway. They couldn't wait for it to open and once again the thoughts of a long, lido-filled summer danced through their minds.

They were going to Rita's to collect some papers for Sandra. Rita was out but she had left the file with Ted. He liked the two of them and found their enduring, insulated friendship uncommon and a little curious. They never fell out, never argued. He'd occasionally overheard them discussing things but more as a debate than an argument. They were both old-headed, he thought, talking about things that he hadn't thought children of their age would be thinking about. Yes, very odd. They were going to separate schools after the summer and he wondered whether their friendship would survive the shift. And, of course, they were getting older; they would start growing up soon. That could be another potential obstacle to staying tight friends. Ted took them into the garden for lemonade and they told him about the wonderful lido gates.

"Oh, yes, the lido. It'll be in the paper tomorrow so I can tell you – it's opening next weekend – only one week to go!"

All the way home they planned their summer. They'd been gathering together all the things that they'd need – swimsuits, trunks, old towels, all sorts of things that they thought they might use in the pool. They moved easily between religious debate and to whether they would need goggles or not. Excitement was also mounting in the small town, and not just amongst the children.

Back home, Judy asked Tim if it was possible that the men who had made the ironwork at the lido might have lived in Sebastopol Terrace and the other Terraces in "the Crimea". Tim thought that it was highly likely. He replied that people lived near their place of work in those days and there had been a foundry behind Alma Park years ago. Judy told Tim of her plan to be blacksmith because she wanted to make beautiful things.

"There are other ways of making beautiful things", said Tim. "You could be a painter or an embroiderer, a tapestry maker, a sculptor, a dress designer."

"How do you learn to do stuff like that?" Judy asked.

"I suppose you'd go to an art college or be an apprentice."

Judy decided that when David went to the seminary she would see if there was an art college in the same town and they could still be together.

*

After Mass the next day Judy waited for David as usual. He had to get changed out of his altar boy clothes and so she waited by the Vestry door. When Judy had first been old enough to go to and from Mass on her own Sandra had disapproved of David going off with her afterwards and had wanted David to go straight home with them after Mass. Joe had said that he couldn't see why David had to go straight home as long as he was home for the big Sunday roast that was their regular Sunday lunch. Judy only ever had a Sunday roast if she and Tim were invited to Rita and Ted's but usually they just had their lunch as if it were any old day. After meeting the Forresters and the Fellowes at the Confirmation ceremony the previous year, Sandra had invited Tim and Judy over for Sunday lunch occasionally in order to get to know the families even better. When her work with Rita took off she didn't need to invite them anymore. She was also hoping that when Judy and David started secondary school they would drift apart. She didn't want David to have any female friends while he was growing up. It would be so easy to be lured from his vocation. This was another reason why she had wanted him to go to the seminary early. She thought about Patrick, Joe's brother and wondered how he had still become a priest even though he'd tasted the pleasures of his girlfriends. She decided that this was because he knew what the sacrifices were and so he was able to make a balanced decision. Perhaps Joe was right. She still didn't know what Joe meant by not wanting history to repeat itself. Sandra and Joe came out of the church and saw Judy standing at the Vestry door as usual. They went over in order to catch David and remind him that he had to be home in time for lunch.

"What are you doing today, Judy?" Sandra asked, making it clear that Judy would not be with David.

"Dad and I are going to Auntie Rita's for dinner and then we're going to the hills for a walk."

Sandra was aware that the Fellowes had a car and felt a familiar pang which she had yet to recognise as jealousy. She and Joe still couldn't afford a car.

"How nice!" Joe said quickly as he saw the look on Sandra's face and knew that the car argument was on its way.

David and Judy wandered off. They didn't have much time so they went to the lido gates and sat on the grass opposite the dolphins and mermaids.

"I've decided to go to art college when I leave school." Judy announced.

"When did you decide that? I thought you were going to be a teacher." David asked.

"No, I'm going to be an artist."

"Are you going to go to the college here?" David asked.

"No. This is the plan. I'm going to see if there's an art college in the same town as the seminary that you're going to and then we can still be blood cousins."

"We've got a problem. This is what I needed to tell you today. I asked Dad about what we'd been talking about the other day, about priests having friends who are women. Dad said that priests aren't allowed to have friends unless they're other priests and they especially can't have friends who are women. He said that when Uncle Patrick was at the seminary they couldn't mix with the people in the town and they even had to go out in threes so that they couldn't be tempted into anything. He said that they couldn't often have female visitors even if they were relatives. So I don't know how we'll stay in touch. I've been trying to think of a way round it."

Judy poured out a torrent of questions,

"But how can there be a way round it if it's a rule? The only way round it would be to break the rules and that would be disobedience and that's a sin. Even more so, because if a rule is specially for priests and they break that rule then it's ten times worse than an ordinary person being disobedient because aren't priests supposed to be better than everyone else? They're not supposed to commit sins because they tell us not to so how can they do it themselves?"

David said nothing. Judy was right. Once he was at the seminary they would never be able to be friends again. Judy broke through his worry.

"What if the rules have changed since your Uncle Patrick was training to be a priest? And you won't be going for ages so even if the rules haven't changed yet they might have changed by the time you go."

David had realised for the first time that being a priest meant that he'd not only be cut off from his family but from his best friend whom he felt he had known forever, even since before he was born. Judy seemed to be part of his very being. He couldn't have expressed this in words because as yet he was not even conscious of it. It was in his heart and in his soul. Sandra had once said to him that something being in your heart and in your soul is how you know the truth. Out of all the children who had started primary school on the same day how come he and Judy approached each other like old friends and stayed by each other's side forever after even though they had never set eyes on each other before that day? So he now had another question that needed answering. Could he have a female friend when he was a priest or even when he was just training to be a priest? He felt that he already knew the answer and a deep sadness ran through him. Judy was quiet too and realising that they were late for their respective Sunday lunches they said a quick good-bye and hurried home.

*

On Friday morning Sandra tested David on his catechism while he tried to eat his breakfast. He knew the definition of God; he knew the meaning of "a dangerous occasion of sin"; he knew what happened to babies who died before they'd been baptised, in fact there was nothing in the little book that he didn't know. But did he understand any of it? Wondered Joe. For heaven's sake, he's only eleven and he's spouting theology and philosophy. Joe remembered when he himself had had to learn the catechism from the age of five. He remembered how the words that God would say to the damned if they died in mortal sin had kept him awake at night. He had tried to grasp the concept of eternity, especially in relation to being "in everlasting fire prepared for the devil and his angels." He'd been sure that when he died he'd hear the words "depart from me ye cursed" and not "come ye blessed of my Father." He now wondered why he'd been so sure that he was going to go to Hell. He'd been a child. He'd never done an evil act in his life; in fact sometimes it had been hard to think of anything he had done wrong when he went to the weekly confession. He remembered telling the priest that he didn't think he'd done anything wrong that week and the suggestion was made by the priest that he had therefore committed the sin of pride. So was he supposed to make up sins? Was he supposed to tell lies in confession? But that would be a sin too, wouldn't it?

Joe realised that Sandra was speaking to him.

"I think David's done so well to learn all this. I remember having these tests when I was at school. I was so frightened of not being able to answer but David won't have that problem, will you David? You know it all so well."

Joe smiled but could only feel sorry for him. He must remember to ask David if any of it worried him but now was not the time.

The teachers were in their best clothes. They wore stern expressions as they instilled into the children how well behaved they must be and how they must answer the priest clearly and correctly. It would go badly for the school and the teachers if the children didn't do well in the test. Every class was to be tested on the dogma of the Catholic Church from the five year olds to the eleven year olds. There was an air of terror permeating the building.

When the priest came into Judy and David's classroom they were surprised to see a jolly, smiling young man who shook the teacher's hand warmly and smiled at the children. His questions were so easy that the children wondered if they were trick questions and that they had missed the point. The priest knew that they were only eleven and questioned them accordingly. He finished by saying that they were wonderful children, that God loved them, before giving them all his blessing. The expected and the reality are so often inaccurate. At lunch time David caught sight of the priest in the corridor and ran after him.

"Father, there are some questions I need to ask you."

"Ah, the Conti boy. I hear that you're going to be a priest. You're going to follow the family tradition. What a blessing God has given to your family!"

David was shocked that the priest knew who he was but he recovered and gabbled out his questions.

"I've got three questions about that, Father. Is there really such a thing as a vocation or do we just choose for ourselves? Why can't women be priests? Can priests have friends who are women?"

The priest's friendly demeanour changed. He looked shocked and confused. He looked more closely at David.

"Those questions will wait, young man, but my lunch will not."

He flounced away down the corridor leaving David not only perplexed but feeling guilty. He'd obviously done something wrong but he'd felt that a priest would be interested in talking about being a priest so what was wrong? Did the priest really prefer to go to lunch rather than discuss these things? He joined Judy and told her what had happened. They felt deflated as they walked home. The priest had let them down.

"You could ask your Uncle Patrick."

"He's still in Africa."

"When's he coming back?"

"No-one knows. He went suddenly and we didn't know he'd gone until he'd gone. He didn't come and say goodbye. The Bishop sent him so it must have been really important."

Chapter 6

This Uncle Patrick, Joe's brother, or Father Conti as he'd been known now for several years was indeed still in Africa. He had started his life as a priest with the certainty that he had a true vocation. He had investigated the pleasures that he would have to give up when he took his vows but he viewed it as research into what he would be sacrificing. When he went home for holidays from the seminary he didn't follow the tradition that trainee priests should continue studying theology and philosophy and spend quiet time with their family. Perhaps they would even go on holiday with their family. It was to be a family and study time. Patrick, instead, went out with his brother Joe and indulged fully in the teenage life of his younger brother before he returned to the seminary. His mother worried about this. Perhaps he'd be lured into the life that he was supposedly leaving behind. She feared the loss of his vocation but not just for his sake. On the other hand, their father approved of this.

"He went to the seminary at the age of eleven. If he misses his teenage years how will he mature and develop? He'll be expected to give people advice and married people at that. How can an eleven year old do that? Because that's where his development will stop. No, he must see something of life or he'll be useless as a priest."

Joe had heard these arguments and remembered them when David, his own son revealed that he wanted to be a priest.

However, Patrick seemed to feel genuinely moved by the lectures at the seminary, about how God has need of men to do His work. He pondered on the idea that Christ has no hands but my hands, no lips but mine, no feet but mine. He could be the carrier of God's love and he was grateful and honoured at the thought that God had chosen him to do His work. Yes, he sometimes yearned for affection, independence, easy comfort. He endured the thought of sharing the love of a woman, the children he could have from that love which was a God-given right, a man's privilege. But he believed that a greater love had lured him to the priesthood. He believed that he was a man of God but Patrick also believed that a priest was greater than a king. A king can give away titles and estates but a priest can call God down from Heaven. Who else could do that? His power would be even mightier than the angels'. His ordination into the priesthood would give him these Godly powers. He would be, as his mother had always told him, the representative of Jesus on earth. God speaks to us through the mouth of His priest. Of course, Patrick knew that this was not pride; it was pride in the office of the priesthood not pride in himself. He ignored the whiff of power he smelt when in later years grown men would break down in front of him and beg God for forgiveness.

The first few years of his priesthood were spent in a small town where he fulfilled his duties with energy and hope. He would visit his parishioners knowing that he was entering their homes in the place of Jesus and presuming that his chats would be encouraging for them. As time went by the worm of disillusionment crept into his heart. He would visit the gaunt women with tired eyes, carrying a crying baby while two toddlers would cling to her skirts whining. He knew they didn't have enough to eat because the husband went out drinking every night. The same man would come to confession over and over again with the same story asking to be forgiven and then, being free of sin, just go and do it all again. He'd been drunk and had hit his wife, shouted at his children, used their money for beer. How many times did he, Father Conti, have to sit in the confessional box explaining to these people that having their sins forgiven included their determination not to do it again? He'd visit the old men with empty eyes who'd given up and were waiting to die; he'd visit those of his parishioners who no longer went to Mass and he'd have to look into their bored eyes knowing that they were waiting for him to leave. They let him into their houses through politeness and even promised that yes, they'd be at church next Sunday. They were all getting on with their own lives. There wasn't much room for a priest.

Patrick then had his big idea. If he could get and keep people into his fold at a young age and instil God into their lives he might be able to stop the rotting away of religion that seemed to happen as they grew older. He would start a Youth Club and stay very closely connected to the boys and girls who came. That would be his world from now on.

The Youth Club was a bigger success than he'd dared to imagine. He mixed with the surly boys and the precocious girls, learning their language and listening to their music. He was gradually accepted by even the most contemptuous leather-jacketed boys. He learned how to chat about motor bikes, music, fashion, films. He brought religion into the conversation in easy ways rather than appearing to give sermons. He was still the tall, good-looking man of his teens and he became popular amongst the teenagers of the town. They would nod or wave to him if he saw them in the street and he exulted in his success. He thought about introducing services at the church just for young people, gearing the Gospel message to their particular interests. He became totally bound up in his new obsession, revelled in his new-found energy and optimism.

When he received a summons from his Bishop he knew that the news of his young flock had reached his superior's ears and he went off to meet him, looking forward to the praise that he knew was his. He wondered what form the praise might take. Would it just be a chat and encouragement or perhaps even the offer of a new position? The chat could not have been more different.

"Patrick, I am sorely disappointed to hear that you are failing in the duties of your sacred office."

He was unable to speak. He had prepared a summary of how he had captured the young people and how he was going to keep them in the church. How could the Bishop be disappointed with that? What was this misunderstanding? There was no opportunity for him to speak as the Bishop launched into his explanation.

"Your duties as a priest are many and varied. You have to say Mass of course and perform the sacraments, all of which you are doing. However, you must also keep in touch with all your parishioners by calling on them, you must visit the sick and especially the dying, give talks in schools, instruct those wishing to convert, prepare meaningful sermons carefully – all of which you have apparently stopped doing. I imagine that you also have no time for theological studies which a priest must keep up. If you consider these studies to be simply a subject to be studied at the seminary then I'm afraid you've missed the point. Without knowledge and piety you will become spiritually blind to the needs of the people in your care. I'm going to send you on a retreat to a monastery which is used for the purpose of bringing a priest back into the fold, a priest who seems to have lost his way. They will help you to find your way back.

You will have time to contemplate the true meaning of the priesthood and you will have time for silent prayer and contemplation. You will have a Spiritual Director to help you in this. You will leave on the sleeper to Scotland this evening. Father Thomas will give you the tickets as you leave."

No mention of the Youth Club, no opportunity to explain its success, no opportunity to describe how some of the youngsters had started asking interesting questions, and how he, Father Conti, the popular priest, answered those questions so well that some of those boys and girls had started to come to his church. Patrick was so shocked that he could hardly think. He was not only hurt and confused but anger and resentment started to flow through him like a red hot torrent.

Chapter 7

The lido held an open evening on the Friday before it was to open for business the next morning. It seemed as if the whole town had turned out to see the Victorian gem. The arcade to the left led to the men's and boys' changing rooms and the arcade to the right was for the girls and women. As the visitors walked down the arcades to the end, the pool came into sight. The tiles on the bottom and sides of the pool were of the same sky blue as the entrance gates and the arcades so that the onlookers felt as if they had arrived at the edge of the Mediterranean. The pool was L shaped so that young paddlers could enjoy the shallow waters of the short side of the L and the swimmers could fly through the long branch of the L. The areas at the side of the pool were paved with the golden stone from the quarry nearby which had been producing stone for the town's houses and offices for centuries. The visitors were silent in their amazement when they first laid eyes on this beauty that had been hidden from them for decades. Fairy lights were woven amongst the branches of the trees at the edge of the paving, giving the whole area a magical quality. Rita and Edward were amongst the invited guests who were taken into what was to be the Lido café for a glass of wine and delicacies. The sponsors, councillors and designers clinked their way through the reception and when Rita and Edward emerged they found themselves face to face with Tim, Judy and David. Sandra and Joe were wandering by the edge of the pool. Sandra looked worried.

"Will it be safe to let the children come here on their own? David wants to come here every day but I really won't have time to sit here watching for all that time."

"There'll be two lifeguards on duty, Sandra", said Edward, "the children will be perfectly safe."

Nora Wilson had joined them with little Billy.

"I'll be here with Billy." She said. "I can get on with my knitting here as easily as at home. I'll keep an eye on them."

Judy had imagined that Sandra would be by David's side at the lido watching over him and fussing, allowing him only short sessions. Tim cut into her thoughts.

"Judy's planning to spend the whole of the summer holidays here. I wouldn't mind coming here myself too when I've got time."

They all agreed that it was a wonderful amenity but wondered if the children would get bored with it after a while. As it turned out they weren't given the opportunity to get bored with it. The weather was kind to them and they did indeed spend most of their time there but only for the three short weeks that were allowed to them.

*

David had been suffering from a sore throat for a few days but hadn't told anyone. He knew that Sandra would keep him indoors if she knew, so he plodded on feeling more strange and achy each day. One day when Judy met David as usual outside the lido he seemed pale and tired. He explained that he'd had a bit of a sore throat and a headache for a while but it was even worse today. Judy suggested that they should go back to his house but he couldn't bear to be indoors on such a lovely day and dragged himself into the pool. They played around with the handful of friends who sometimes joined them but David went to stand at the side for a while, saying he didn't feel well.

"You've got summer flu!" shouted little Billy Wilson. "It's infectious!"

They jumped out of the water and played around as if David had the plague. He smiled and played along with them for a while until he used all of his remaining strength to climb out of the pool. He whispered to Judy that he felt very strange as if he was in a dream, nothing seemed real. He reached out to her as he collapsed. The lifeguards and several adults who'd been taking advantage of the Lido on their day off from work ran to him. An ambulance was called.

"Did he bang his head?" Someone asked.

"Is he still breathing?"

"There isn't any bruising or blood." Said another

"Make way, please."

The men from the ambulance checked on the apparently lifeless body but David was still breathing. They looked round and asked if anyone knew what had happened. Judy told them that David had a sore throat and headache but that was all. Little Billy Wilson said David had flu but Judy said that they didn't know that, they were just guessing. The men put David gently onto the stretcher and carried him to the back of the ambulance. Judy followed.

"Can I come too?"

"Are you a relative?"

"No."

"Then I'm sorry but you can't. Can you give me his name and address?"

Judy did so. They were acting very quickly and urgently. This made Judy frightened and she felt herself trembling as she managed to write down David's details on the pad.

The ambulance took David away while Judy stood silently watching until it disappeared. She felt helpless and bereft, but taking little Billy Wilson's hand they went to the changing rooms, gathered their belongings and wandered slowly back to Sebastopol Terrace as if in a trance. What could she do? Tim was at work but Nora Wilson, Billy's grandmother, was on hand for if Judy needed anything. Judy had offered to look after Billy that day so that Nora could have a break and she was surprised to see them back so early. Billy rushed in, excited by the ambulance, telling Nora what had happened. There was no option but to just wait until they could find out what was wrong. Judy couldn't settle so she went home next door and lay on her bed. She couldn't wait for Tim to come home so that she could tell him the dreadful news.

*

Very early the next morning there was a sharp rap on the door followed by the doorbell. Judy and Tim had barely started their breakfast and they both jumped at the unexpected, unusual sound so early in the day. Tim went to the door. A man was standing there blocking out the early morning sunshine.

"Mr. Forrester?"

"Yes?"

"I'm Doctor Harris from the Public Health Authority. May I come in please?"

Tim stood aside to let the doctor in wondering what on earth this man wanted. Perhaps he'd come to the wrong house. No, that couldn't be it because he'd asked for him by name. Weak rays of sunshine emerged as the man unblocked the sky and moved into the house.

"Good morning, Mr. Forrester and this will be Judy? I believe you are a friend of David Conti and I have a list from Mrs. Conti of all the people that David has been in contact with over the past few days. That is, as far as she knows. You see, I'm very sorry to have to inform you that David Conti has Poliomyelitis, Polio. As you probably know, this is a very serious condition and infectious."

A chill wrapped itself round Judy. Numb, she moved into another universe. The moon drew the oceans from their beds. The earth disintegrated. In this strange world that Judy now inhabited she heard the doctor continue speaking. He seemed to be talking from the depths of the seabed, muffled and hazy.

"Judy must stay in isolation and must not leave the house or mix with other people for at least two weeks and you must call a doctor immediately if she has any of these symptoms."

He handed over the list.

"We thought we'd never see a case again when the vaccine came along. This has taken us by surprise. We're gearing up for a possible epidemic like the one we had a few years ago. That was caused by contaminated water in swimming pools. You might remember that all the pools were closed for quite a long time. The lido's closed and the water's being analysed."

This was said in a rush as the doctor left to go to the next person on Sandra Conti's list. Those comments only made Tim's anxiety worse. The long, terrifying wait began. Of course, Judy could not have visited David even if she hadn't been in isolation herself. She moved to the window and saw a man walking his dog, a lorry drove by, a woman pushed a pram. How can ordinary things still be going on when the earth has collapsed? Doesn't the rest of the world know that the world has stopped? Tim walked over to her and squeezed her shoulder.

"We'll get through this just like we got through your mother dying."

"She wasn't my mother, she was your wife." Judy spat out. She seemed wild, fighting against tears. Tim didn't recognise her. The sensible, loving Judy had never acted like this before.

"I don't remember her, I've never known her. I don't have a mother. But I do have a friend and I do know that he's dying. That's what I know."

She raced out of the room. Tim sat down in a daze. It appeared that Judy had no recollection of Agnes who had loved her so much and tended to her for three years in her gentle way. Surely Judy would have a vestige of memory, perhaps not of the physical features of her adoptive mother but a vague memory of tenderness, an aura around her that had come from Agnes? Judy had never mentioned Agnes and nor had she ever asked who her real mother was. Tim had not realised that this was because Judy had no feelings for Agnes. The huge sadness that had engulfed him when Agnes died attacked him again and he sat with his head in his hands.

Judy lay on the bed and did what she and David often did. One would concentrate on the other and seem to enter their mind, leaving thoughts there for them to read. Until Judy had read the magazine article they hadn't known that they were practising telepathy and getting quite good at it. They would discuss the next day what had come into their minds the night before and match it against the thought that had been sent. They felt that they knew when it was a message and not just their own thought. She lay on her bed and closed her eyes. When her body felt calm and relaxed she concentrated hard on David and called on God to save him, her prayers were desperate pleas for his life. She sent love, but finally she sent a demand that he must not die. She realised that if David died God would lose a future priest so how could God let him die? A wave of relief spread through her. She knew he would not die.

*

Are there any words that can describe the fear of losing one's child? No, there aren't. So Sandra was silent. The Conti house was silent. Both parents' misery wove itself into their beings. Their bodies expressed their feelings better than any words could. Sandra's eyes were red from crying, black from lack of sleep. She wore no make-up and her hair was dragged off her gaunt face. Father O'Brien called in and was shocked to see the pretty, vivacious woman that he knew turned into a dishevelled wreck. Joe looked no better but it was Sandra's lack of make-up and dull hair that stood out and made her look so different from usual. He searched for words of comfort.

"Leave this to God. Put your suffering on the altar and God will listen."

Neither Joe nor Sandra spoke. They had been visiting David in the hospital but were not allowed in the room. They had watched him through a porthole window in the door. He lay in what appeared to be a giant metal tunnel with just his head showing. They were not allowed in, not allowed to stroke his hair, not allowed to give him tender words of encouragement. The only people to go in were nurses wearing masks who checked gauges but didn't seem to notice David himself. It broke their hearts. A doctor walked up the corridor to where they were standing.

"Mr.and Mrs.Conti? I'm Doctor Burton."

He had shaken their hands with a look of deep compassion in his eyes and invited them into his office. He had explained the situation to them as clearly as he could to lay persons.

"There are two types of polio – paralytic and non-paralytic. We are doing tests and watching David closely to see which type he has. If it is non-paralytic and if he has it mildly then it could be just like a very bad dose of flu and he will have a complete recovery with possibly just a few after effects. The paralytic type speaks for itself. There is also the danger, and I'm sorry but I must tell you this, that the disease can be fatal."

Perhaps it would have been better if the doctor had given the information on the possibility of death at the beginning of his explanation and not the end because then Sandra and Joe would have gone home with the possibility of "like a very bad dose of flu" ringing in their ears instead of the words "the disease can be fatal". They had returned home to their separate despair. Father O'Brien had arrived soon afterwards and neither of them was in the mood to talk. Joe decided to go into the kitchen and make a pot of tea. He couldn't remember when they'd last eaten but he wasn't hungry. He wished Father O'Brien would go but he couldn't bring himself to ask the old priest to leave when he had come to help them. The only problem was that Father O'Brien rarely helped, usually said the wrong thing, was basically out of touch with the times. As Joe was carrying the tray into the living room he heard their lowered voices and stopped in amazement and confusion. Sandra was weeping uncontrollably.

"This is God's punishment. I know it is. It must be. He's punishing me for that dreadful thing I did. Taking my son as punishment."

Father O'Brien replied quickly.

"No, no. You mustn't think like that. It was a long time ago and you and I both agreed on the best course to take and we said that it was all over and we need not speak of it again."

Joe crept back into the kitchen and put the tray down. What on earth had Sandra ever done that was so horrendous that she could imagine that God would punish her with the death of her own son? It was clear that Father O'Brien knew of it, presumably from the confessional? It appeared that they had discussed it and he had advised on a course of action. Joe remembered that after Sandra had given birth to David, the doctor had warned them that it would be dangerous if Sandra were to become pregnant again. The birth had been difficult with complications that could have been life threatening. Joe had tried to persuade Sandra that in those circumstances, surely the church would allow contraception? A young couple couldn't be condemned to live celibate lives together because that would seem to be the only answer. She had been adamant that it would be a mortal sin and did not dare to go against the ruling.

Suddenly, one day, she agreed to use them. Yes, that would be it, Joe thought with relief. She must have discussed it with the priest and he had given her an exemption from the rule. Could priests do that? Joe didn't know. So now, he presumed, Sandra was thinking that because she had prevented having children then her only child would be taken away as a punishment. He could see the logic in that even though he disliked that view of God as being full of revenge like some medieval despot. She'd never told Joe why she'd changed her mind but then he'd never asked her.

Joe's idea was not, in fact, the truth of the matter. Yet again Sandra had not told Joe the true story. He hadn't asked why she had changed her mind and so she was grateful that she hadn't had to lie to him. She had explained the situation to her neighbour who at that time was an older woman with four children. Sandra thought she might help her to decide what to do. The neighbour put it to Sandra:

"So imagine that you don't use contraception because of the Church's ruling and then you get pregnant. You can't have an abortion because that's also against the Church's ruling. You die in childbirth. What's the first thing that Joe will do? He'll have David and a new baby. What can he do? He'll go and get another woman. He'll be re-married within the year. You'll be quickly forgotten and all because you followed the rules of a group of old men."

That evening, Sandra said that she had re-considered and they should use contraception. Joe took the tray into the living room, hoping that the tea was still hot. He would be loving and tender towards Sandra and they would bear the fear for David together. Joe came into the room in time to hear Father O'Brien say to Sandra:

"You know, Jesus will have David either way. He will either make him His priest when he's grown up or perhaps he's getting impatient and He wants him now."

Sandra stared at the priest.

"What? You think David's going to die?" She wailed and ran out of the room.

Joe was speechless. There were so many things that he could have said in response to the priest and most of them not nice things, but he just sat in silence with his tea staring at the person who had simply made matters worse by thinking he was making them better.

*

Judy lay on her bed and concentrated on David. She could see his face clearly and fell halfway to sleep, dreaming of him. He was walking towards her across a vast barren desert. He was soaked in sweat and his walking was getting slower and slower, his legs getting weaker and weaker as he tried to reach her. Judy, herself, was high on a hill watching him coming, urging him to keep going, don't stop, keep going, if you stop you'll never have the strength to get started again, keep going! She woke bathed in sweat and with tears on her cheeks. Tim was standing over her with a look of fear and horror. He could see the sweat and had heard her call out. He took her temperature and went through the symptoms. No, it had just been a bad dream. A nightmare had caused it. How he wished Agnes was here. Would a woman know how to calm a child better than he could? Why had Agnes died so young? He felt surrounded by death and sadness. Judy had lost her previous, unusual wildness and bitterness and clung to Tim.

Two nights later, Judy and Tim were woken by an uproar in the road. They went to the window and saw an ambulance hurtling round the corner into Inkerman Terrace. Nora, from next door, was rushing up the street in her slippers and dressing gown. After a while she walked slowly back down to her house. Joe opened the door.

"Nora, what's happened?"

Nora went in and sat down heavily and wearily. The clock showed two o'clock.

"It's Billy. He had a high fever, sore throat, headache, nearly all the things on that list the doctor gave us. His arms and legs had been aching all day but they thought it was from gardening. While he's been stuck at home in isolation he'd been helping his Dad in the garden, weeding and planting and that. But when he got the throat and the fever in the night they had to call the ambulance."

She looked at Judy, small, pale and frightened.

"Are you all right, love?"

"Yes, thank you, Mrs. Wilson." Was all that Judy could say.

They all went back to bed but none of them slept. Judy remembered the beautiful lido gates. The mermaids wrapping the dolphins in their tails now seemed like evil viruses tying up children. Kidnappers, killers. What would happen to the lido now? If it was disinfected and re-opened would anyone ever go again? They'd loved it so much and it had betrayed them. She entered David's mind again and fell into a fitful half sleep. She was standing on the shore. David was swimming strongly towards her through a massive ocean when a great wind arose. It was deafening, building up sheets of water into twenty foot waves. His strokes became weaker, he went under, was thrown up again, went under again. Judy screamed at him above the uproar that he must keep going, keep going, keep going. If he didn't keep going he would drown. Don't go under. He looked up at her on the shoreline and his strokes became stronger. He swam nearer and nearer, almost there. Tim was by her side again, wiping her forehead.

"Did he get to the shore, Dad?"

"It was a dream, Judy, another nightmare."

Rita and Edward visited Sandra and Joe but there was nothing they could do. They reported back to Tim and Judy that the Contis were allowed to go to the hospital every day but could still only look through the window in the door and were not encouraged to stay long. But Judy kept her faith and thought hard of David every night, getting into his mind and urging him on.

The parents of the children who went to the same Primary School as David and Billy asked Father O'Brien to organise a special Mass for the two boys who were so dangerously ill. The children who had been with the boys were still in isolation but the rest of their old primary school friends and many others went to pray for the boys. The parents arranged the church. There were to be no lights on in the church. It was lit by candles only and huge arrays of sweet smelling flowers lined the aisles. It was too beautiful, too much to bear. Silence seemed to have come to the town. There was no gossiping, no shrill bursts of laughter, not even any arguments. The town seemed to be holding its breath.

*

Sandra and Joe walked through the corridor of the hospital to the room where David lay entombed.

"He's gone! My David, where is he?" Sandra screamed.

Doctor Burton came running down the corridor.

"Mr.and Mrs.Conti! I'm so pleased to see you and so sorry that I couldn't reach you before you saw that the room was empty. Please come into my office."

They followed Doctor Burton into his office waiting in tense silence for whatever news he had.

"It's good news! Very good news! David has non-paralytic Polio and he doesn't appear to have too severe a dose. He has also rallied significantly in the last few days. We usually wean children slowly off the iron lung but his breathing is strong and he won't need to go in it again. However, I must warn you that he's been through a lot of pain and fever and is very weak. He will need considerable rehabilitation when he leaves the hospital."

Sandra and Joe felt the flow of relief through their bodies and the great weariness that they had kept at bay washed over them.

"This rehabilitation, Doctor." Joe asked, "How do we do that? What does it entail?"

"We have a special rehabilitation centre for children which is part school, part body building. When the child is ready and able, they'll have lessons in the morning so that they don't fall behind at school and then they they'll do more manual style work in the afternoon to build up their strength, always outside in the open air."

"And how long will he have to be there?" Joe asked

"It all depends on his progress. Some children spend a year there, some only a few months."

Sandra looked horrified. "A year? Months? But he's starting at Saint Francis in a few weeks time."

"Oh no, I'm sorry, Mrs. Conti, that's not possible."

"So where is this centre, Doctor?" asked Joe.

"I'm afraid it's a good twenty miles or so from here in a rural part of the county. "The Oaks Open-Air School". You might have heard of it?"

Sandra was horrified yet again. She'd heard of this place and had presumed that it was a place for "bad boys" as she called them or children with some kind of difficulty, "not all there" as she would say.

Doctor Burton continued. "It's an excellent centre. Very good reputation. It improved the lives hugely of those children caught up in the big polio epidemic a few years ago. Without it those children would be leading very different lives now."

The pleasure of David's survival was now tainted by this new change to come into their lives. Would this nightmare never end? Is there always good news followed by bad news? But in reality, they realised, that under the circumstances this was all good news, surely?

"So now, I imagine that you'd like to visit David?"

"We can visit him?" Gasped Sandra.

"He's in a private room at the moment just off the main ward. I'll take you."

Sandra cried and hugged David while Joe stroked his hair. He was very pale and weak but he was alive and going to survive.

"We came every day to see you but they wouldn't let us in the room. We just had to look through the window in the door." Sandra croaked through her tears.

"But Judy came to me every night", David said.

"What? She couldn't possibly have been here. You were very ill and highly infectious."

"She did. She kept telling me not to give in, to keep going."

Sandra marched out into the main ward. A nurse was sitting at the table.

"My son has told me that he's had a visitor every night. He's convinced that she was there. He couldn't have had a visitor, could he, when his own parents weren't even allowed to visit him?"

The nurse smiled. "No, of course he didn't have any visitors. You are the first people to see him. He'll have been dreaming or he could possibly even have been hallucinating. The painkillers are very strong and sometimes they have strange effects. He was calling someone's name. It was Judy." The nurse laughed. "We thought that perhaps it was his dog! Children always miss their pets when they're in hospital."

Sandra didn't reply but walked slowly back to David's room. She was furious. Everyone knows that boys call for their mothers, not some random girl. Young men, dying on the battle field always call for their mother, not their dog, not their friends. She was insulted, humiliated. Of course, this had nothing to do with David or his feelings for his mother, she concluded. It wasn't David's fault. No, it was that girl, that girl who'd wriggled and wormed her way into David's head like a parasite. Sandra would make sure that that girl kept well away from him in future. There would be no more Judy. David would recover, go to Saint Francis, go on to the seminary and fulfil his vocation.

"Are you all right, Sandra?" Joe was shocked at Sandra's pursed face. Had the nurse given her bad news?

Sandra said that everything was in order, that the nurse had reassured her that no-one had visited. She started to fuss round David allowing herself to fully take in the news of his recovery. They said goodnight to David and as they passed the nurse's desk Sandra stopped.

"I think it would be preferable if only adults were to visit David. I think his friends would make him tired. He needs to rest."

"Oh no, Mrs. Conti, they wouldn't make him tired. It would do him the world of good if his friends could visit. The children are always brighter after a friend has visited. Adults can be very serious when they visit a sick child but friends of their own age just treat them normally and it helps to bring them back to some kind of normality."

Sandra realised that she'd have to find another way of keeping Judy away. When Sandra and Tim got home, the news that their son was recovering lightened the atmosphere between them and they ate and slept properly for the first time in weeks

Rita called the next day to find out how David was. She was slightly reluctant to call as she'd had no news of how serious David's case was. She knew that seven children altogether had been taken ill, David and Billy and five more from outside the town but that was all that she knew. She was relieved by the reception she received from Sandra and was invited in hear the news. It was a relief for Sandra to talk about David's recovery, to hear it all explained out loud again just as the doctor had described it. She was pleased for another reason too.

"If you see Judy, please tell her the good news but could you also tell her that no children are allowed in the ward? I know she'll want to see him but I'm afraid it's not possible."

"I'm surprised" replied Rita. "Surely there's no chance of infection at this stage? Did the hospital tell you why they won't let children visit? I would have thought that it would do David good to see his friends."

"Perhaps it's just too early. Have more tea, Rita. It's so good to see you. I'm grateful to you for coming. I must catch up with our work. Tell me all the news. I'll be back as soon as things settle down."

"You mustn't come back to the charity until you are sure that everything is back to normal. We miss you of course but my goodness, what you've been through!"

After leaving Sandra's, Rita went along to Tim's. Judy was there and Rita told her and Tim the good news.

"I knew it would work." Judy was jubilant.

"What would work?" Asked Tim and Rita simultaneously.

"My telepathy. I worked on David every night and I could feel it working."

"That's very interesting." Grinned Tim. "I didn't know you practised telepathy! How long have you been doing that?"

"David and I have been doing it forever but we didn't really need to learn it, it was just there. It was something we did automatically and then I read about it in a magazine and realised that was what we were doing and that it had a name."

Rita and Tim smiled. Just the night before, Rita and Ted had been talking about David and Judy. Ted had always thought that they were a curious pair and Rita wondered what he'd think about this latest revelation.

"The bad news is though, Judy, that apparently children aren't allowed to visit the hospital so I'm afraid that you won't be able to see David for quite a long while. When he leaves hospital he's going straight to a special place where they'll make him strong again."

Judy stared at Rita, unable, unwilling, to accept what she'd just heard.

"But he's starting at Saint Francis in a few weeks time. If he's doing so well why can't he just go straight there?"

"It appears that the doctor has told them that polio leaves you very weak and achy so you have to have treatments and therapies to help you get your strength back."

Judy drowned in a hopeless emptiness. She sat back with the glazed expression of the defeated. Rita tried to bring her round. She asked her about Saint

Catherine's Convent school which she'd be starting in a few weeks time. Judy answered the questions but from a distant place. She was no longer excited about her new school. There'd be no David waiting for her at the bandstand or at Saint Ambrose. They hadn't even decided yet where they would meet on their way to their new schools. There was no point to anything now. Then Rita offered to take her into town to buy the few bits and pieces of uniform and equipment that she still needed. Rita said they'd make a day of it and have lunch out in the restaurant of the splendid new department store that had just opened.

"My friends have told me that it's just like Selfridges in London. I haven't been there myself yet so I think you and I should go and explore it."

Tim was taken aback by Rita's sudden thoughtfulness and kindness. Taking Judy into town for her school uniform had never been Rita or Judy's idea of a good day out. In fact Tim felt that Rita had become a little aloof over the years. Tim was relieved when Judy replied politely. She thanked Rita and said that yes, she did need some more things for the new school. They decided on a day and Rita got up to go. Tim walked her to the door and thanked her for her help. She just smiled and left.

    The local newspaper had reported that seven children had contracted polio and analysis had proved that the water in the lido pool had been the source of the virus. Tim had had no news as to how little Billy Wilson was doing as he hadn't seen Nora since the fateful night when the ambulance came for Billy. He presumed that she was staying round the corner with her son and family. That evening, after Rita's visit in the afternoon, Tim heard movements next door and rushed round to see if Nora was back.

"Come in, Tim, yes I'm back. Billy's out of danger! He's only had a light attack and he's recovering really well just like David. They're both in the main ward now and he's tickled pink because his bed's right opposite David's. But you'll know that, won't you, because you'll have been in yourselves?."

"Oh Nora, I'm so pleased for you and the family. What a relief for your son and his wife, and for you too, of course. It's a pity they won't let children visit though because Judy's very keen to go and see David and…"

Nora interrupted him.

"Won't let children visit? What made you think that? Of course children can visit. Billy's friends from school and his cousins have already been."

"But ….." Tim hesitated. "That's great, Nora. It must have been a mistake. I'll go and tell Judy now. Thanks, Nora."

Tim stood outside the house. How strange that Rita had said that no children could visit. It could have been a simple misunderstanding. But he felt that there was something else. He stood there puzzled. It didn't make sense. Judy saw him through the window and came out.

"What are you doing, Dad?"

"I was just thinking. But great news! Billy's going to be ok and Mrs. Wilson says that children *can* visit the hospital. I was just wondering how Auntie Rita got it wrong or I imagine that Mrs.Conti told her, so, in that case, it's Mrs. Conti who got it wrong. But she's been through so much worry that I imagine it's easy to make mistakes when you're in that state."

Judy was relieved to hear that she could go to the hospital but she was equally puzzled. Something didn't feel right. She felt that it wasn't a mistake, this wasn't a misunderstanding. She felt a disturbance inside her like an oncoming earthquake slowly making its way towards her. She'd been aware that Sandra hadn't liked her in the past but she thought that was all over now. The two families had become friends and she'd felt that Sandra's animosity towards her was well in the past. In fact, she hadn't seen much of Sandra recently and had no reason to believe that she had gone back to disliking her. No, it must be as Tim had explained. The poor woman had nearly lost her son. Sandra clearly doted on David and would have been shattered, utterly devastated, if he'd died or become paralysed. When Judy thought about what Sandra had been through she decided that she was being a bit selfish and should feel pity for Sandra not suspicion. She put all that behind her as she prepared to go to the hospital and gathered the gifts together that she'd been collecting for when David recovered. Because recover he would, she'd known that.

They arrived at the hospital to find Sandra and Joe already at David's bedside while the Wilson family were sitting opposite around little Billy's bed. Billy was animated, enjoying being the centre of attention but David lay limp and pale. All of a sudden David hoisted himself up and his lovely face lit up, the lines from the pain he'd suffered easing. Sandra looked to see what had effected such a sudden change and to her annoyance saw Judy and Tim approaching. In the same way, Joe noticed the sudden look of shock and then anger that flashed across Sandra's face and he looked to see what had caused it. He was pleased to see them and wondered why Sandra wasn't pleased too. Surely it would cheer David up to have a friend of his own age visiting and clearly that had happened. As they approached down the ward, Nora Wilson called.

"I'm glad we sorted that mix-up out. It would've been a pity if you hadn't come to visit."

"And that's thanks to you, Nora!" Tim called back.

Joe asked what the mix-up was.

"We'd been told that children couldn't visit the hospital but Nora knew that we could because Billy's friends and cousins had been."

Joe knew that Rita had been to see Sandra so any news that Tim and Judy had been given would have come from Rita who would have had it from Sandra. Was Sandra against Judy and David's friendship again? Now that the two families knew each other and had become close friends he thought that her dislike for Judy had dissipated. He'd never understood it in the first place. He decided not to ask who had told them that they couldn't visit but he'd certainly have this out with Sandra later.

"The main thing is that you're here now and you're very welcome. David was hoping you'd have come yesterday but now we know why you didn't and thank goodness Mrs. Wilson was on hand to put you right."

Sandra said nothing apart from asking Judy not to sit on the bed. Joe immediately told Judy to take his chair and he went off to find two more chairs.

Judy and David spoke quickly in low voices.

"It worked. I did it every night."

"I know you did. I saw you in my room every night."

"You actually saw me?"

"Yes. One night we were in a sort of desert and another night it was an ocean and every time, you were standing there telling me to keep going and don't give in. You saved my life, Judy, because I felt so ill and weak I was just going to give in and sleep but I would have slept forever, I would have died. It was as if I was actually being given the choice of dying as a way out of the pain. I knew I didn't want to die but I just hadn't the strength not to give in until you arrived and then you gave me the power to keep going."

David was talking in a rush but so low that the others couldn't hear. However, Sandra caught bits of it and her resentment and fear grew. The girl was a witch. She must somehow keep her away from David.

"That's enough now, you two." She said. "David will get very tired with all this talking.

Joe laughed.

"He's looking better than we've ever seen him. This is obviously the best medicine for him!"

Sandra bridled. She wanted David all to herself. Now, after being so close to losing him, her total devotion to him was becoming manic. She would only release him from her hold if it was to the Church. The bell sounded warning visitors that visiting time was over and Sandra and Joe, Tim and Judy reluctantly gathered their coats and bags, hugged David and made their way to the door. As they walked past Billy Wilson's bed they stopped to wish him well and Billy's parents and Nora left with them as the bell warning visitors to leave was sounded again. Nora was staying with her son for a while and they all went their separate ways at the hospital gates. On their way home Joe asked Sandra why she had told Rita that children couldn't visit the hospital, knowing, hoping, that Rita would pass this on to Tim and Judy. Sandra feigned surprise.

"Oh, so that was my fault, was it? Why would I have said that? I haven't been able to think straight since David became so ill so if I did say it I have no recollection of it and have no idea why I would say it."

Joe was aware that Rita knew people at the hospital through her charity work and so he pondered over the possibility that perhaps Rita had been told the visiting rules by someone she knew. They had made a mistake and given Rita the wrong information. It may not have been Sandra's doing at all. He felt guilty and ashamed that he'd blamed her, especially when they had both been through so much together. He apologised to Sandra and decided to make amends. They would have their evening meal at the new restaurant that they would be passing on their way home. They would celebrate David's recovery. Sandra was so relieved that the blame had passed her by that she burst out in to tears. Joe as usual, mistook the cause and motivation of the tears, put his arm around her and they headed for the restaurant.

In the meantime, Tim and Judy were strolling home.

"Why do you think we were told not to go to the hospital?" Judy asked Tim.

"Someone just got it wrong and said that children weren't allowed in. Sometimes children aren't allowed in at visiting times for various reasons."

"No, we were kept out deliberately."

Tim believed that she was right but decided not to go along with it.

"But who would do that? Why would they do that?"

Tim realised that these were the wrong questions because he too suspected that it had been done deliberately but he didn't want to hear the answer. Rita hadn't actually said that Sandra had told her. He'd just presumed that that was where the information had come from. There was no reason as far as he could see that they would be kept out on purpose. He decided that there must be a sensible explanation. Someone had simply made a mistake.

"Mrs. Conti doesn't like me, she never has."

Tim decided to diffuse this straightaway. They were overwrought. They'd been living in anxiety for weeks now. First, they'd had the fear of David's death or paralysis, then the fear that Judy might have contracted the disease, watching for symptoms all day and night, and now they, or at least Judy, had the fear that she was somehow being pushed out of the life of her best friend. He countered Judy's suggestion that Sandra didn't like her.

"Why on earth wouldn't she like you? You've been friends with David for years, you go to their house, David comes to our house. If she didn't like you she wouldn't let David do that."

"But she'd have to give a reason why she didn't want us to be friends and there isn't one."

"But Mrs. Conti's a good friend of Auntie Rita's now and they work a lot together so surely she'd be happy for her son to be friends with Rita's niece?"

They were home now and Judy said no more. She knew in her heart that for some as yet unknown reason, Mrs. Conti did not want Judy and David to be friends. She lay on the bed with her hands behind her head and toyed with the problem. If she was a boy would it be different? Was it because she was a girl? Judy remembered the conversation she'd overheard once between the Contis when Sandra had complained that boys of David's age usually had friends who were boys and then Joe suggesting that they might make different friends when they went to different schools. Then there was the question as to whether priests could have friends who were female. Judy decided that this was definitely the reason for Mrs. Conti's behaviour. She felt better that this was the reason and not that Sandra actually disliked her. She had known that David wanted to be a priest ever since she met him on that first day at Primary School. She wondered if she should tell Mrs. Conti that she knew that priests couldn't have friends who were girls but David wasn't a priest yet so it was ok. No, she decided against it. She'd leave well alone and be on her guard.

Tim realised that Sandra and Joe would want to spend as much time with David as possible so he arranged with Joe that he and Judy would call in to the hospital just for short visits every other day. Joe was grateful for Tim's understanding because the situation with Sandra's opposition to their visits was becoming unbearable. But then the time finally arrived for David to go to "The Oaks" to bring him back to full strength. It was Judy's last visit.

"This is what we should do." Whispered David. "We'll write to each other every week and post the letter on Fridays. Then we'll get them on the same day and be reading them at the same time. It'll be like talking. That'll give us something to look forward to. I want to hear about Saint Catherine's and I'll tell you what goes on at "The Oaks." Shall we do that?"

"Good idea. And I think we should go on with making up stories where the characters and buildings have to be the names of football teams. When we've got enough I'll make them into a little book and I'll put drawings in as well."

David groaned.

"I'm no good at that and we've done so many I don't think there are any left."

"Ok, I'll do that and I'll send you one every week. Do you know yet how long you'll be away?"

"No, but they say that I'm doing well so it might only be for one term. I'm doing some exercises every day holding on to the rail at the end of the bed. My left leg doesn't behave properly and it's much weaker than my right one. They say I'll have to work hard on it or I'll be left with a limp. I want to go on playing football so I must get it right."

"You will."

"I can't believe I won't see you again until Christmas."

Chapter 8

Patrick, Father Conti, who was still in Africa, had no idea what was happening to his nephew. Post didn't get through very often and he was miles away, both physically and mentally from his family. He was sitting in the evening thinking back to his time at the monastery in a remote part of Scotland where his Bishop had sent him. His Spiritual Director had been Father Anthony, monk and priest. Father Anthony always approached people who were sent to him with kindness and compassion. He knew that severity and harshness would only increase their burden and even build up the resentment which may already be there. Gradually, Patrick uncoiled from his confusion over the Bishop's treatment of him and gave his side of the story. He knew that the Bishop would have sent a report to Father Anthony and Patrick wanted his counsellor to have the full story.

"Patrick, the Theology that you learn in the seminary is just the beginning, just the rudiments. A priest who is going to be effective must continue the study. Your sermons will reflect this. A sermon is the priest's opportunity to show his parishioners how to live well in this ever-changing world and not fall into the emptiness of the world's temptations. Pius X1 said that the word "cleric" should be synonymous with "scholar". He said that even among the absorbing tasks of his charge the priest should still continue his theological study with *unremitting zeal*. Preaching *off the cuff* is really a waste of everyone's time. An old Abbé once said that a priest who gives up study becomes worldly in his tastes."

Father Anthony looked at Patrick's tired face; he could see that their hour was up, much more would be counter-productive.

"You now have the time to catch up with your study and you have the silence here to contemplate how to include your ideas for bringing young people into the church with the many duties which you already have. God bless you. Go now and we will meet again tomorrow."

Patrick, sitting in the dark in Africa, remembered the simple room that he'd had at the monastery with its white walls and crucifix, single bed, wardrobe, desk and chair. He remembered the regular simple meals; the humility and kindness of the monks. He remembered the view of the valley and trees from his window and longed to be away from this heat and sweat, the mosquitoes, the poverty.

He'd followed Father Anthony's direction, catching up with his studies, contemplating his future as a priest and then the awful realisation dawned that perhaps there was another choice, a choice that he'd never even known was there– he could stop being a priest. There was the idea that once you had been anointed as a priest you could never not be a priest. "Once a priest always a priest." But in fact, he thought, he could actually stop practising as a priest even if the seal of the priesthood was still within him. That alternative had not offered itself to him before but he started to play with the idea. What work would he do? Would he marry? Could he remain a Catholic under the circumstances? Would he want to? Would the Pope excommunicate him? Father Anthony became aware of Patrick's crisis and offered him a way out.

"Our Order has a mission in Africa. They're desperately in need of another priest and have asked us if we could help. It's only for a year, by the way. If you went over there, the complete change of scene would take you out of yourself and perhaps enable you to see things in a new light. You could think through and plan what you'd like to do in the future while at the same time performing a very useful and necessary service for our Brothers in Africa."

Patrick thought it over. He knew he couldn't bear to be a Parish Priest again. Other posts in the Church were taken by priests with more experience than he had so what was there for him to do? He would go to Africa, give himself the year to decide on his future. His Bishop gave his permission for him to go, relieved that he wouldn't have to deal with Patrick's return. The Bishop had foreseen that sorting out a new position for him in the Diocese would have been difficult. Everything seemed to have fallen into place.

But that year, rather than providing him with space to think overwhelmed him with the unbearable heat, tiredness, constant illness and non-stop demands. He'd had neither the time nor the energy to sit quietly in the sunset pondering his future. There wasn't even a sunset. Now, recovering from yet another fever, he was sitting on the veranda of the Rest House for Missionaries away from the searing heat. It was already two years since he'd arrived and this was the first time that he'd had time to think. He knew that he was already broken mentally and spiritually but now his body had given way too. The strong rugby player of his youth had been sucked out of him. He made up his mind on one point – he would go home. This place didn't suit him. He was just a burden rather than a helper. What he would do when he went home was still unknown to him.

*

Neither Patrick nor David knew of each other's illness and convalescence as they both sat in the darkness feeling their bodies aching and their minds exhausted by the uncertainty of their future. David had been taken to "The Oaks" by ambulance with Sandra and Joe following in a friend's car. They were shown round the Home which had been a grand Victorian mansion built by the same industrialist, Sir William Alexander, who had built the Lido. How circles do enjoy themselves. The look, feel and smell of the place had transformed the once elegant house into the cold blankness of an institution. But the gardens were another matter. A huge vegetable garden provided the house and a market stall with every kind of vegetable that it was possible for them to grow. A wooden gate at the far end of a walled flower garden led to the banks of the river, the same river that Judy and David had strolled by for so many years, which had listened to their philosophies and chuckled with their jokes. David swallowed hard and shut his eyes tight so that his mother wouldn't see that he was upset. He'd listened to his mother's lectures about being brave, about changing his underwear, about doing what he was told. He was now torn between wanting his parents to go and wishing they could stay. It turned out that there were not many children in the Home at the time; in fact the Matron was worried that the place might have to close. As soon as his parents left he was asked what he would like to do. He would start the routine the next day but for now he could make himself at home, rest in his room, go to the Common Room or the library. He was free until tea-time. Would he like to be with the others? No, he needed some quiet time alone to orientate himself. The Matron decided that he was old enough and seemed sensible enough to be left on his own for the hour before tea as that seemed to be what he preferred.

He went straight to the library which was still a splendid room but minus the leather-bound books collected by the original owner. He sat at one of the many writing desks and started his first letter to Judy. His mother had given him stamps and paper to write home but with his pocket money he'd bought more so that he could write secretly to Judy. It had been made clear that Judy would not be visiting. Sandra and Joe still didn't have a car much to Sandra's chagrin and were reliant on friends lending them theirs. Tim didn't have a car. As far as Sandra could see, there was no way that the little witch with her magic tricks would be bothering her son again. When he came back home they wouldn't even be at the same school. Saint Francis had excellent after-school activities and she would make sure that David made full use of them.

*

When Rita went shopping she didn't go into the local town, preferring the city of Westerbridge, a few miles further down the line. Her trip there with Judy was on the same day as David's departure - a beautiful, sunny day with no hint of the oncoming autumn. Rita decided that before they did anything they would go to the restaurant in the new department store for coffee, returning there for lunch when they'd bought all the things that Judy needed for her new school. Judy rarely went beyond her own village and town and her new interest in art allowed her to see buildings differently from how she'd seen them before. There was the magnificent Victorian Town Hall, gardens and a park with a huge bandstand, far more elaborate than the one in her own Alma Park. Her favourites were the offices that had belonged to shipping companies where the river was at its widest and had been deep enough to take ships. The ornamentation made her stop and take in the suns and moons, ships, crests and the names of all the far-away countries that had done business with this small city in its wealthy past. Rita stopped and waited while Judy gawped at the beauty of these places that most people took for granted as they passed by. Now that Judy was growing up Rita was becoming more inclined towards her, she even felt a growing fondness for her. When Judy was a baby Rita had felt no interest in her, sometimes feeling guilty that she didn't help more but unable to feign any interest. Did that make her less of a woman? But now that Judy was on the verge of being a woman herself, Rita realised that Tim would be unable to take the place of a mother in the way he'd managed so far. Rita decided that from now on she would be the woman in Judy's life, the one who would explain the mysteries of womanhood to her.

The new department store was beyond even Judy's imagination. Large glass doors were opened for them by a commissionaire who even performed a little salute as they entered. Judy was delighted and then amazed by the marble pillars, the chandeliers and the sweeping staircase. They swept up the stairs to the restaurant where ferns were reflected in brass framed mirrors, red velvet chairs surrounded circular tables and little nooks held tables for two. She sank into the deep carpet as she and Rita were shown to a table by a waitress in a black dress and white lacy apron. Judy gazed at a shiny machine that made frothy coffee, the silver trolley holding the cakes, the efficient, courteous staff and drank in an ambience that she'd never experienced before.

"Auntie Rita, is there an art college in Westerbridge?"

"There's a university but not an art college. Whydo you ask?"

"I want to go to an art college but it would have to be in the same place as a seminary."

Rita had to choke down a laugh. She couldn't think of two more diverse places.

"Why would there have to be a seminary?"

"So David and I can still be friends."

Rita didn't reply. She didn't know a lot about the Catholic Church but she knew enough to know that that would never happen.

They found all the things that Judy needed and then wandered through the quaint city until it was time to go back to the station for their train home. This old city was a favourite of the Guide Book writers who found each phase of history unrolling through the streets, the buildings and place names, making their job easy- "an outstanding view of the Romanesque Cathedral can be found on Caster Hill where the remains of a Roman fort still guard the cobbled alleys of this delightful city with its medieval squares, Georgian Avenues and Victorian town houses. This city which is, in fact, only the size of a small town ......" and so on they would rapture. But, Judy, too, had caught this rapture.

*

"The Oaks"

Saturday

Dear Judy,

Mum and Dad have just left and Matron let me come into the library to write to you. There's no-one else in the room. You'd love it. It's got wood panels and oil paintings. I'm going to come in here a lot. Matron says there aren't many other people here. It's a massive house. There's a big dormitory but I've been given my own room. It's small with just a bed, a wardrobe, a desk and a chair. It's like the room Uncle Patrick described that he had at the monastery in Scotland. I love it because the window looks out onto the garden and the river's there at the bottom. It's the same river that we walk along. If you walked along the bank for twenty miles we could meet or you could pinch a canoe!

Sunday

We had a sort of Service in the Hall that used to be a Ballroom and then we had a short walk. I'm the oldest here and the others are worse off than me. Some of them have got things like metal casings on one of their legs to help them to walk but it seems to make it more difficult for them because the metal's so heavy. Some of them are in wheelchairs.

Monday

Because there's no-one else of my age here I've got my own tutor. We went in the Library (my favourite room) and did some Maths and English. I got tired really quickly so we didn't do a lot. My tutor's called Mr. Jackson and he seems really nice. He limps too but that's from the war not polio. He said that I won't get so tired as time goes on and he'll make sure that when I go to Saint Francis I'll be up to the right level. I hope he's right. I don't want to be put in a babies' class.

Tuesday

We started on Physiotherapy this afternoon. They've given me some exercises to do like at the hospital and they said that when I'm a bit stronger I can help in the garden.

Thursday

I was going to write a page every day but I didn't have time yesterday and I was too tired by evening. We have to hand in post on Friday mornings so I'll have to finish now. How are you? I do hope you've written.

David

2, Sebastopol Terrace

Saturday

Dear David,

      I'm thinking about you especially today because I know you were bothered about going to "The Oaks" and what it would be like. I hope it's good or at least ok.

I went to Westerbridge with Auntie Rita today to get stuff for school. It's the most beautiful place I've ever been to. (But I haven't been to many places!) When you're better we must go there. It's only two stops from here on the train.

Sunday

I went to Mass at Saint Ambrose as usual and Father O'Brien asked everyone to pray for you and little Billy. It felt wrong leaving the church and not waiting for you and then not going to the bandstand and going along the brook and all the things we've been doing for years. I just went home but couldn't think of anything to do.

Monday

I can't believe that I start at Saint Catherine's next Monday. I'm a bit nervous. Some people who go there say it's dead strict but others say it's nice so I suppose it just depends on what sort of person you are as to whether you like it or not. I'm bored stuck here with nothing to do. I could go and see other people from school but I just don't fancy it.

Tuesday

I've been doing a lot of gardening, mainly just weeding. It gives me something to do. I need a really good description of where you're living so I can imagine you there.

Wednesday

I tried to write one of those Football stories today but it just wouldn't come so I won't be sending one this week. Perhaps you're right and we've used them all up.

Thursday

I'll have more news next week because I'll have been at Saint Catherine's for a whole week!

I hope you're getting better very quickly. It's so boring here without you.

Judy

"The Oaks"

Tuesday

Dear Judy,

I was so happy to get your letter even though I knew you would write. You said you wanted a good description of where I'm living so you could imagine me here but we could do even better than that. I know it's twenty miles away but is there any chance you could come and visit? Mum and Dad can't bring you – it's something to do with using some else's car but I don't see what that has to do with giving someone a lift. Anyway, is there any other way you could get here (apart from walking or canoeing!)

I had the best day so far yesterday when I went in the pool – it's called the Hydrotherapy Pool. It's funny that a pool made me ill and a pool's going to make me better. We do exercises in the water and then swim or walk in the pool afterwards.

Mr. Jackson's lessons are good. He's a nice, gentle sort of person but his eyes are really sad. Perhaps he saw awful things in the war. We did a lot of Maths. yesterday and he was pleased and then we did some English Language. He said we can start Latin next week!

It's not the day for sending post but one of the nurses said she's going into town this afternoon and she'll post it for me.

Don't forget to think of a way of getting here. Fly on a goose's back!

David

2 Sebastopol Terrace

Wednesday

Dear David,

It was so nice to get a letter from you when I wasn't expecting one. Uncle Edward has already offered to take me to see you but your Mum told Auntie Rita about the rule that only relatives can visit so I won't be able to come.

I've had two days at Saint Catherine's and it wasn't too bad. I'm still getting the feel of it. We've had our first Latin lesson so we'll soon be able to speak in Latin to each other and nobody will know what we're talking about.

Judy

David went to look for Matron. The door to her office stood open, as usual and she called to David to come in. He felt awkward but knew that he must ask about the rule that stated that only relatives could visit and not friends.

"But that's not the case, David. Anyone can come and visit you. You know the saying "the more the merrier" and that's true. It'll cheer you up if your friends can come. What made you think that friends couldn't come?"

"My mum told my friend's Auntie that only relatives could come."

The matron looked quite shocked but then recovered and just said,

"She must have just made a mistake, misread the rules or something. No, you tell your friends that they'll be very welcome."

David wrote to Judy as soon as he was free. It had all been a mistake. She could come with her Uncle Edward. No need for a canoe or a goose.

When Judy asked her Uncle Edward if it was still ok for him to drive her to "The Oaks" because it had turned out that Sandra's information had been wrong and friends were allowed to visit, Rita and Edward both had the same thought. That's twice they'd been given the wrong information from Sandra, first about visiting at the hospital and now about visiting "The Oaks." Why was Sandra doing this? Why was Sandra preventing Judy from visiting when she and David were such good friends? Should they tell Sandra that she was wrong, just act as if she'd made a mistake, like before, or should they have it out with her and ask why she was doing it? Rita decided that the latter would be difficult as Sandra was about to resume her work with Rita. On the other hand,

David was Sandra's son and Rita supposed that she had a right to know who was visiting him. She thought over the problem and knew exactly how to deal with it.

Now that David was out of danger and she could only visit him at weekends, Sandra had decided to go back to her work with Rita's Charity. It would keep her mind busy and stop the fear and fretting that had ruled her life for so long. Rita welcomed her back and insisted that they have a coffee before getting down to work. Rita first of all asked Sandra for the latest update on David's progress and then as she stood up to pour the coffee she looked at Sandra and smiling said,

"Sandra, we have some super news! It turns out that you must have been given the wrong information about the visiting rules at "The Oaks". It's not only relatives who can visit but friends can go too! Edward has offered to take Judy to see David but we don't want to intrude on your time with David so we'd like you tell us when the best time would be for us to go."

It passed through the minds of both women that this was the second time that this had happened but no mention was made of that. Rita passed the coffee to Sandra and kept a smiling, enthusiastic face. No blame apparent.

"Oh dear, I wonder how that happened." Said Sandra looking down into her coffee. "Visiting times are

Saturday and Sunday but we can only go on Saturdays because of not having a car. So if you could go on a Sunday that would be nice for David to have visitors on both days."

Rita wondered at the effort Sandra must have had to make to say that. She knew how much she doted on David and how she'd been without him for weeks now and had faced the possibility of losing him, her only child. She had been through so much that Rita softened towards her and thanked her very much. She would ponder later on what was going on between Sandra and Judy.

Late September sunshine feathered through the trees into Judy's bedroom as she wrapped up the gift she'd made for David. She'd done a little drawing of the bandstand and brook and another of the river and their barn. The journey to "The Oaks" didn't seem to take very long to Judy as she sat in the back of the car entranced by the thought of the two hours ahead. Rita and Edward said very little as they passed through the villages and dappled lanes that would lead them to the Home. They didn't know what to expect and hoped that Judy's hopes were not too high.

As they drove down the tree-lined drive the three of them gasped when the huge mansion came into view. It didn't have the grim, forbidding aspect that Rita had imagined but it was a symmetrical harmony of soft golden stone, glowing in the sunlight.

David was waiting by the massive oak door. He looked taller and thinner than Judy remembered even though it was a relatively short time since she'd seen him. His thick, black hair had grown long since his illness, medical treatment being more important than worrying about how to get a barber to him. As he moved towards the car they noticed that he was limping and had picked up a walking stick which had been propped against the door. Judy was first out of the car and flew to him. They stood close, facing each other but unable to speak. Their silent reunion was broken by the matron's appearance and after introductions were made she suggested that David should show his guests round and then there would be tea and biscuits when the bell rang.

They wandered round the house noting the original carvings, beautiful plaster work and panelling which had all been betrayed by the utilitarian furniture, metal filing cabinets and notice boards which transformed the once beautiful vision of the original architect into something ugly and banal. It had become an institution, lacking in funds to preserve its splendour, needing the space for activities for which it was not designed. The vegetable garden and flower garden had escaped the needs of the school and had retained their Victorian flavour. As they wandered, David told them about the routine of the place; his one-to-one lessons with Mr. Jackson, the hydrotherapy and physiotherapy, the little jobs in the garden that he'd started doing. They were surprised to discover that he seemed to be enjoying his time there and Rita and Edward relaxed as they heard the bell and the little quartet strolled to the old Orangery where visitors were served their tea and biscuits. David asked Rita if he could show Judy where the garden sloped down to the river. Rita was acutely aware that Judy and David hadn't had any time to themselves and said that they could go if they didn't end up in the river. There was relieved laughter as they stood up, promised not to fall into the water and walked slowly down the smooth lawn towards the lower terrace, through the gate and down the steps to the river bank. They sat on the bench by the river with views across fields for as far as the eye could see. It was still warm, a dragonfly zigzagged along the bank and an arrowhead of geese flew overhead. It was perfect but a layer of sadness lay over the scene. Judy turned to face David with tears in her eyes. His black eyebrows were perfectly arched over his deep brown eyes and his hair had an almost blue sheen.

She had never noticed that before.

"How much longer will you be here?"

David looked at her. Her delicate nose tilted slightly at the end and her hair was a mixture of chestnuts and sunshine.

He had never noticed that before.

"I don't know how long I'll be here. They won't say. It's just my leg that's bothering them. It still aches so much."

They were quiet, intensely aware that their relationship had somehow changed. He noticed that a little white feather had become entangled in her hair and gently unravelled it. He'd never touched her hair before and he was shocked by how soft it was and by the desire he had to gather it up in handfuls and bury his face in it.

"Don't ever leave me again, David." Judy whispered through her tears.

"I won't. I promise."

"But when you're a priest …….."

David had a pain in his throat from holding back the tears. He took hold of her hands,

"We'll work something out. We're blood cousins, remember?"

Rita and Edward were walking down the slope when they caught sight of them sitting very closely together, holding hands and speaking intently. Rita stopped and held Edward back. "Let's give them a bit more time."

Chapter 9

The best thing about Saint Catherine's, in Judy's opinion, was the new art block. The school roll had increased dramatically and new extensions had been added in the past few years. The art block was different from other new building work from the point of view that it stood alone, separated from the main buildings by a short path and a circle of trees. This was Judy's haven on Wednesday afternoons when an Art Club met after school. The pupils were encouraged to do just whatever art work they themselves wanted to do. The Art Club gave the freedom that Judy craved in her desire to create, born on that day when she first laid eyes on the lido gates. She'd forgiven the lido for David's dreadful condition, realising that all misadventures come from humans and their activities. There is nothing else ever to blame.

Her first painting was a recreation of the figures on the lido gates drawn from memory. After the class had left the Art teacher looked through the paintings and drawings of this first year class and became intrigued by the quiet, intense new student who quite clearly had an artistic gift. Judy Forrester, mused Miss Stevens. She didn't know anything about her and had heard nothing from the other teachers who always became excited when a little Einstein joined their class. An inspired student like this girl might join your class just once in a lifetime and she decided to encourage her as much as she could. Other departments in the school often had students going to University whereas her art department was considered to be merely something akin to recreation. If the school needed time for rehearsals or special assemblies it was always the art class or the music class which was cut. The very qualities that made humans deserve the epithet "humane" were the very sessions which were least valued. This was her *bête noire* of which the other members of staff were only too well aware.

Rita and Edward had given a camera to Judy for her last birthday and she had used up a whole film at "The Oaks" with a view to making a series of paintings, including a portrait of David if she could manage that. She decided to ask Miss Stevens for some instruction on portrait painting at the next meeting of the Club.

When the photos were developed Judy was very pleased with the one of David. She'd been taking photos of the river and the fields and he'd been unaware that she'd turned the focus onto him. There was a little zoom on the camera and she caught a close-up of his face. He was looking seriously straight ahead but with a detached look and a sadness that came through his eyes. Judy realised that to catch that look would take a very talented artist but she was determined to try and hopefully with the help of Miss Stevens. She was moved by the sad look on his face and wondered what he'd been thinking about at that point. She took the negative to the Chemist's in the town and asked for two enlargements, one to take to the Art Club and one to have in her bedroom.

*

Sandra was agog to hear about Rita's trip to see David and could hardly wait for her Monday morning session working with Rita. Rita knew that Sandra would want as much information as possible and that's fair, thought Rita, as he is her son after all. She didn't make her wait or have to ask but launched straight into her account.

"Oh, I must tell you, Sandra, that David was in such good spirits yesterday and very kindly showed us round the house and the grounds. We were so pleased to see him looking much better than we'd expected. And "The Oaks"! What an amazing place. Edward was very taken with the architecture. We were so glad that we'd had the chance to see it. And the matron, what a lovely woman!"

Sandra noted that there was no mention of Judy and was determined to find out what new tricks she'd played.

"What did Judy think?"

Rita was careful in her reply.

"She thought it was an amazing place too. We'd bought her a camera for her birthday and she certainly made good use of it – all those beautiful views of the meadows and the river and that lovely old Orangery. She's becoming a good little photographer."

Sandra was thinking, so, no mention of David and Judy going off together on their little jaunts like they did at home. No, Rita was too sensible to let them go off on their own. She was satisfied that Judy hadn't had the opportunity to play any of her voodoo tricks.

Rita didn't mention that in two weeks time they'd be going again. Edward had been reading the biography of Sir William Alexander, the Victorian industrialist who'd lived and worked in their own town but had rested and played where David was now living. Edward wanted another look at the place now that he knew about the man who'd not only lived in, but had designed that interesting place. Lucky for Judy that the place had sparked this interest in Edward. Again it seems that the needs of one were met by the different needs of another.

Sandra told Joe that evening that Rita and Edward's trip to see David seemed to have gone well. Joe was relieved and didn't mention the "mistake" over the visiting rules. In fact, Joe had some very good news that he knew would please Sandra even more than it pleased him. Since David had been at "The Oaks", there seemed to be less to do and in the evenings Sandra had buried her worries by watching the new television they'd recently bought. Joe had taken the opportunity to go into the little spare bedroom that he'd made into a study and catch up on a backlog of work. He was an accountant and the small company that he worked for had become popular not just in their own town but further afield. They needed more staff to accommodate the flood of work and while the new staff settled in Joe brought the backlog up-to-date. The Board appreciated Joe's extra work which he had done in his own time and they also appreciated his thoroughness, his calm demeanour, his honesty, punctuality and on and on as the Director listed Joe's good qualities at the board meeting with the result that now that the firm was expanding they would like to promote him to senior accountant with the appropriate pay rise and his own office. Joe had kept the news for the appropriate moment and decided that Sandra seemed to be in a good mood that evening after her day working with Rita. Of course, he was right. The higher status and pay rise were exactly what would keep Sandra on an even keel for a while, especially when he mentioned quite casually that they would soon be able to have a car. From the depths of despair to the heights of elation. Would anything in the future ever match their journey to Hell and back? All was well. How could anything ever go wrong again?

*

Judy took her photos to the Art Club and propped up the photo of David. Miss Stevens noticed that all the pupils were already working on their chosen subjects so she was free to spend some time with Judy. She walked over and her eyes fell on the photo of David.

"Oh, my goodness, what a handsome young man! Is he your brother?"

"No, he's my friend."

Judy felt a blush rise up into her face but Miss Stevens either didn't notice or chose not to.

"I want to paint his portrait but I don't know where to start."

"Well, what a lot of people don't realise is that our eyes are actually half way down our head and not near the top as they appear to be."

Judy looked shocked and they both laughed.

"Divide the face into segments. I'll write it all down for you and draw you a diagram. Is this the only copy you have? It would be useful to draw the segments onto the actual photo."

"No, it's ok. I've got another one at home." Judy felt the blush spreading again and kept her head down.

Miss Stevens gave Judy the information and suggested that she should work in charcoal first, quickly and roughly to loosen up. She could then use pencil and be a bit more detailed. But do these exercises several times.

"The painting will come later, if you decide you still want to paint it. It might look more dramatic just in charcoal. But that's up to you."

She smiled and went to help another pupil.

Judy looked closely at the photo. It was a face she'd known since she was five years old. She felt that she knew it as well as her own face. She could almost draw it without looking at the photo. She thought about how she'd blushed and how talking about David had always been easy but now even the thought of him felt different. Their drastic separation caused by the illness had somehow unleashed a new dimension into their relationship. It was a fear of losing one another and an even greater appreciation of their friendship. By the end of the session she had five charcoal and two pencil drawings. Miss Stevens looked through them and immediately picked one out.

"That's the best one. And you've never done portraits before? You're a natural, Judy. I'll spray it so that it won't smudge. Have you inherited this gift? Are your parents artistic in any way?"

"I don't know."

"You don't know?" Smiled Miss Stevens.

"I mean, I'm adopted so I don't know if my real parents were artists."

Miss Stevens was at a loss for a moment. She felt awkward and intrusive but decided to be matter-of-fat about it or she would risk embarrassing Judy too. She went on,

"Sometimes it's not inherited it's just picked up by what's around you as you're growing up, so are your adoptive parents artistic?"

"My adoptive mother's dead and I've never seen my Dad draw so I don't know."

Miss Stevens wished she had never started this conversation. She felt that she'd intruded into this girl's life in an awfully clumsy way. But it increased her interest in Judy all the more.

"Perhaps it's just your own gift. I hope you're pleased with this portrait. I've never seen anyone take to portraits so quickly."

It was soon time to leave and Judy packed her equipment, left the studio and wandered home. She took her time, deep in thought. She arrived back at number 2 and made a decision.

"Dad!"

"Yes, in the kitchen."

Judy walked into the kitchen.

"Dad, I want to know who my real parents are."

"Where on earth has this suddenly come from?" Tim asked, turning away so that the panic wouldn't show.

He picked up the tea towel and started drying the already dry plates and putting them away, bumping into the cupboard door in his haste.

"I want to know who I come from, who I am."

This was the moment Tim had been dreading. He knew he should have told her when she was little and she would have just grown up knowing. It would be a shock now and he feared the repercussions.

"Can we talk about this another time? I'm busy at the moment."

"There won't ever be another time and you're not busy."

Tim didn't recognise this calm, steely person standing in front of him. He remembered the one time when her mood had suddenly changed and that was also to do with her mother when she'd shrieked that Agnes was not her mother. He knew the truth would hurt her but he didn't know how she would react. In fact, he was frightened.

"Why do you need to know? Don't you want me to be your Dad anymore?"

"Dad, you'll always be my Dad even though you're not my real Dad. This isn't about leaving you and going to live with my real parents. They mightn't even be alive, for all I know. I just want to know who I am."

She was nearly crying and the commanding presence had left her. Tim put his arm round her and led her into the living room and sat down. Judy faced him and demanded,

"You know, don't you? You know who they are."

"This will be a shock, Judy. Please prepare yourself for a shock. Yes, I know who your mother is and I think I know who your father might be but I've never met him. We were going to tell you when you were little but when your Mum, well your adoptive Mum, died when you were only three, everything was just a mess and as the years went by I couldn't do it. Then I thought I'd tell you when you were grown-up. I wasn't going to keep it from you, honestly, Judy."

She was now on the brink of finding out who her mother was and the excitement and fear made it hard for her to breathe.

"Your mother is the person you know as Auntie Marie."

"What? The nun? How can a nun have a baby? She's still alive. Why isn't she here looking after me? Why is she in a convent when I'm here?"

Judy's shock turned to tears. Her own mother had refused to be her mother. She cried until she was empty. Tim sat by her and let her cry it out.

"Judy, let me explain. She didn't abandon you. I'll tell you the whole story. Your Mum – oh dear, I don't know what to call her now. Your adoptive Mum, Agnes, my wife, couldn't have children. We both wanted to have children and decided that at some point we would adopt. Agnes' younger sister, who you called Auntie Marie, lived with us. She'd been talking about becoming a nun but she was too young to enter a Convent so she got a job at the local library until she was old enough. But then she started to see a young man from the library, not someone who worked there but a customer who went in regularly and who she'd got to know quite well. Agnes and I were really pleased that she was getting a bit more experience of life because we'd felt that she was too inexperienced to know that she wanted to be a nun for the rest of her life. She never brought this young man home to meet us but she always told us when she was meeting him and where they were going. Agnes felt responsible for her and often asked her to invite him home. But she never did. She only referred to him as Freddie so we didn't even get as far as knowing his full name. We thought that eventually it would all work out and Marie would bring him home if they got serious. After all, they were very young; there was no hurry. But then one day when she was only seventeen she announced that she was having a baby but absolutely refused to tell us who the father was. She said that she wouldn't have married him anyway and so there was no need to involve him. I said that he had to take responsibility for his child but she just wouldn't budge. She went away to stay with one of their cousins a long way from here. The cousin explained to her friends and neighbours that Marie was a widow and she gave her a ring to wear."

"Why would she do that?"

"People are hateful to women who have babies when they're not married and the child gets called nasty names too."

"Is that why she didn't tell anyone who the father was? So that people wouldn't be nasty to him?"

"No, it doesn't work like that. The men don't get blamed. But that's another story. Because Marie was so young and had no husband to support her she had no option but to let you be adopted."

"But couldn't she have gone on living with you? You could have supported her. We could have all lived together here."

"At that time we didn't have much money and the house is too small and to be honest, Marie was in a bad way. She was very religious and couldn't come to terms with what she'd done. According to her Faith she'd committed a very serious sin by having a baby when she wasn't married. We offered to adopt you. You were Agnes' niece, a blood relative, family. Marie was grateful and as happy with the arrangement as she could be given the circumstances. She stayed on living with their cousin and we took you to see her as often as we could, bearing in mind it was a long way from here. But it always upset her and when Agnes died Marie entered a convent."

"But when Agnes died she could have come back here and looked after me and been my mother."

"We couldn't have lived together in the same house because we weren't married. People would have presumed that we were living as a married couple and that we were living in sin, as they like to call it. I think she went into a convent as a penance because she thought she'd committed the biggest sin and this was her way of atoning for it."

"So all of this happened because of what other people might do or say?"

"That's what it sounds like but it wasn't like that."

"Wasn't it?"

Judy felt as if she'd been swiped off the face of the earth. The earth seemed to stop and detach itself from her in the same way that she had been thrown into a strange universe when she'd first heard the news that David had polio. She didn't know whether she was angry or sad or at least pleased that she knew who her mother was. In a trance, she left the room. She'd just started a new school, her best friend was far away, her own mother was still alive but ignoring her. She couldn't take any more. She lay on her bed and concentrated on David. She needed to tell him. She needed his help. Now that she knew what his room looked like she could transport herself there and will him to listen. She poured out the story to him and eventually fell asleep. A letter arrived from David ahead of his usual weekly letter.

"The Oaks"

Dear Judy,

    I had such a strong dream about you on Wednesday night it made me wonder if everything was ok. You were wandering through a thick forest, looking behind trees and under stones as if you were looking for something. Then a young woman in a long white dress appeared in the distance. She was glowing and might have been an angel but I don't think she had any wings.

    I know you're coming here on Sunday but I can't wait that long so please write back straightaway and tell me.

David

2, Sebastopol Terrace

Dear David,

    Yes, I've had some terrible news but I don't really know whether it is terrible or not. Or perhaps it's good news. That sounds daft but I'm all mixed up. I really need to talk to you about it. I can't write it in a letter. I'll tell you on Sunday.

Judy

*

Tim hadn't known how to deal with the aftermath of the news. He had no idea how Judy had taken it. All he knew was that she had gone very quiet and hadn't spoken about it again. She must be digesting it, he thought, he should leave it for a while. He decided to tell Rita that Judy now knew about Marie and perhaps Rita would know what to do and possibly talk to Judy about it. He just didn't know what to do. If Agnes hadn't died he imagined that they would have explained it all to Judy by now. That had been their plan. He'd let Agnes down, he'd let Judy down. He remembered that it was this Sunday when they were going to "The Oaks" again. An afternoon with David might cheer her up. The house was quiet. Judy was in her room, no doubt drawing, which was her passion now. It occurred to Tim that Judy was alone a lot now because in the past she had always been with David, either there at number 2 or at David's, although that was not so often, or they'd be out walking by the river or in Alma Park. Should he encourage her to make new friends?

Nora Wilson knocked at the door and bustled in, her cheerful exclamations brightening up the dullness. Little Billy had been transferred to "The Oaks." She was so happy that he was out of the hospital. He needed a lot of help with his legs though. He was still very weak. She gabbled out all the news in a flurry of optimism while Tim filled the kettle and asked her to stay for a while.

"I've come round to tell you the news but I wanted to tell Judy as well that I'm sorry we won't be able to give her a lift to see David because the car will be full. I'm so sorry, she must be missing him. They were attached at the hip, those two; it must be hard for her to lose her little friend like that and for such a horrible reason."

"It's ok, Nora. My sister and brother-in-law have taken her and they're taking her again this Sunday so it's not so bad."

"Well, isn't that kind of them! Judy's at Saint Catherine's now, isn't she. Such a good school. My niece went there and she did so well…. ……"

And so Nora Wilson filled the kitchen with her chat and her bits of gossip. Tim basked in the normality that Nora had brought back into the house but deflated when she returned to her busy life back in the real world.

Judy came down and started to help with the dinner as they usually did at that time in the evening. He was relieved. Were things back to normal? He asked if she wanted to talk about what he'd told her the other night but she said no, quite sharply. Did she blame him, he wondered, had he betrayed her in some way, would she forgive him? These thoughts raced round his head but he knew that it wasn't the right time to ask. An awkward, laden silence filled the room and he was glad when the time came for her to go to bed. He knew he needed help but couldn't work out who or what might provide it. They'd always had such a good relationship. Was that now at an end? He couldn't bear it.

*

Rita and Edward picked Judy up the following Sunday. Tim hadn't had chance to tell Rita that Judy now knew that Marie was her mother and he hoped that Judy wouldn't say anything about it until he'd prepared Rita.

On arrival at "The Oaks" Edward asked Matron's permission for him to have a good look round the house from the point of view of it having been Sir William Alexander's house rather than its present use as a rehabilitation centre. He showed her the biography of Sir William that had several chapters devoted to the house. The request was not unusual for the Matron as architectural students quite often requested permission to visit the house. David and Judy were glad that Rita and Edward were not going to be with them for the whole afternoon and they went down to the river bank. David was no longer using the walking stick but his limp was quite pronounced. They settled on the river bank and David looked closely at Judy.

"What's the terrible thing that's happened?"

Judy burst into tears suddenly, surprising both David and herself. He put his arm round her and pulled her into him. He found himself kissing her cheek as the tears flowed. He'd always thought of Judy as the strong one of the two and he was disturbed by this new frailty that he'd noticed the last time she'd visited and now today. She stopped crying and sat up straight looking at the river and the meadows beyond. Then she turned and looked at David.

"I know who my mother is."

She told the whole story to David who sat in silence until she'd finished.

"David, I'm so mixed up. I'm glad I know who my mother is but I don't want it to be her. If it was someone I didn't know or someone who was dead it would be easier but I can't bear the thought that she could have been my mother and chose not to be."

"But your Dad explained all that."

"I know, and I understand all the reasons why she did what she did but it still hurts so much."

"Why did your Dad decide to tell you this now? I remember you saying once that you weren't bothered about knowing."

"That's true but that was a while ago. Someone asked me about my parents and it set me off wondering. I asked Dad if he knew who my parents were and I could tell straight away that he knew. I really want to meet her, to see her, to talk to her but she's buried in some convent that doesn't allow visitors unless there's a good reason. I don't know whether they know that she's had a child so I can't really apply to see her, claiming to be her child. I don't want to mess her life up even though she's messed mine up."

Judy cried again and David pulled her into him again, kissing her hair.

"What shall I do, David? I can't stand it."

"Write to her."

"What if the Mother Superior reads everyone's letters like they do in prison or when you're in the army in a war?"

"You needn't say that you're her child because when you say that you're her sister Agnes' daughter Marie will know exactly who you are but anyone else reading it will think you're her niece. You can pretend that you're writing to her for some reason or other."

"But what reason could I give?"

"You could say that you've just started at a convent secondary school where you're doing a project on orders of nuns and you'd like her to describe convent life."

"David, that's so brilliant. I'll do it."

Her face brightened, the load dropped away and she grabbed his hand and kissed it.

He laughed and a lock of hair dropped across his forehead.

"Miss Stevens was right. You are very handsome." Judy blushed as she complimented him.

"Who the heck's Miss Stevens and how can she have seen me?"

"She's my art teacher. She saw my photo of you. I was drawing a portrait of you from a photo I took last time I was here."

"You took my photo? You cheeky thing! So where's this handsome portrait?"

"I didn't bring it."

David was laughing, pleased to have been called handsome. He was aware that their relationship was changing. He'd felt it the last time Judy visited and he'd wanted to touch her hair. He'd felt a certain shyness at the thought of her next visit but coupled with a longing to see her. But it all felt right.

Rita had happened to look out of the library window just as David had pulled Judy towards him and kissed her cheek.

"Ted, come and look, quick."

"Mmm?"

By the time Edward had moved to the window David and Judy were just sitting next to each other talking. Rita told Edward what she'd seen. He was nonplussed.

"Well what can you expect? They're at that age, aren't they? Growing up."

Rita stared at Edward.

"But they're only twelve years old. Twelve year olds don't have those kinds of feelings."

"I think you'll find that they do. I always thought that when they started growing up they would either drift apart or come together and now I think we know the answer."

"But what about all this business about David wanting to be a priest?" Rita said.

"Yes, indeed. Perhaps this is exactly why Sandra keeps trying to keep them apart."

"But, Ted, surely she wouldn't have thought about that until they were much older."

"Well, I've always thought that their relationship was quite strange. They both seem a lot older than they are in some ways and then suddenly they'd seem like children again."

"Perhaps because we haven't had children ourselves we don't know these things."

"But we've been children ourselves. We can remember being twelve. Did you ever have a crush on a boy?"

Rita smiled as she remembered the paper boy. She'd hide at the side of her bedroom window so that she could watch him without being seen. She'd watch him as he went along one side of the road, cross over and go all the way along the opposite side. She could remember him clearly and she could even remember his name and yes, she'd be about twelve.

Edward caught her smiling and said,

"Yes, I thought so! And I can remember my first crush too. But you were my biggest crush."

Rita looked at Ted in astonishment. It seemed a long time since they'd spoken affectionately to each other. She looked at Edward and said seriously,

"You were mine too."

They looked over at each other and smiled. The natural affection that Judy and David showed to each other seemed to have rekindled a sensitivity in Rita and Edward that years of familiarity had blunted.

The bell for tea and biscuits rang and they met up with Judy and David in the Orangery. Judy seemed a lot brighter than when they'd arrived. She wondered whether it was time for her to give Judy the woman to woman talk that Agnes would have given her at this age. Tim certainly wouldn't be able to do it but he'd never mentioned such things to Rita or asked her to stand in for the missing mother. It was time to leave and she heard David ask Judy if she was really going to do what he'd suggested. Judy said yes, definitely, leaving Rita to wonder what they'd been talking about.

When Judy got home she realised that she couldn't write to Marie because she didn't have her address. While Tim was in the kitchen she rifled through his desk looking for his address book. She jumped when he suddenly appeared and asked her what she was looking for.

"I'm just looking for the address book. I'm not looking for the millions of pounds that you've got hidden here."

Tim smiled.

"Well, you certainly won't find that in there or anywhere. You won't find the address book there either- it's on the book shelf. Anyway, who are you writing to? Oh no, just a minute, you're not going to write to Marie are you?"

"Why not? I won't say I'm her daughter in case they don't know she's had a child. Do they know?"

"I don't know so it would be better not to say."

"I know they're strict. Can she have letters?"

"Family can keep in touch but mainly if something happens in the family, like someone dying."

"I could write and say that I'm Agnes' daughter and I've just started secondary school and it's a convent and I'm interested in convents."

"Please don't write to her." Begged Tim. "She used to get so upset when we took you to see her. It would start it all off again for her."

"I don't just want to write to her. I want to see her, meet her, get to know her."

"I really do understand, Judy, but it's just not possible."

Judy went to her room and wrote to David. There was no hope, she wrote, of ever meeting her own mother.

*

The following Saturday when Sandra and Joe visited David there was another blow in store for them.

Doctor Burton from the hospital was waiting for them.

"Mrs. Conti, Mr. Conti."

He shook hands with them and led them into the office.

"David's recovery is satisfactory apart from his left leg. If he left here at Christmas he would almost certainly never lose the limp. But if we could continue treating him with physiotherapy and hydrotherapy for a while longer then I feel sure that we could strengthen the leg to such an extent that the limp would be eliminated."

Sandra felt her eyes fill with tears. Her life was empty without David. She went through the motions of working with Rita and playing the housewife with Joe but her heart, as ever, was with David. But could she shorten David's recovery, condemn him to limp for the rest of his life just so she could be with him? Even Sandra was not that selfish. Sandra and Joe felt that they had no option but to allow the doctors to continue working on David in the hopes that he would return to being the athletic football player, the keen swimmer, the tree climber, that he'd once been.

Doctor Burton was relieved at their decision and added that David could enjoy a few days at home over Christmas although he was worried that once they had David back home they might decide not to take him back to "The Oaks." Joe was adamant that they would return David for his treatment. In fact, he and Sandra were very grateful for all the help that David was having. He looked at Sandra for confirmation but she could only nod.

When David heard the news he didn't say much. He was disappointed but keen to reclaim the full use of his leg. Since the diagnosis of Polio he seemed to have become slightly detached. He only came alive again when he was with Judy or writing to her.

They strolled gently round the garden and Sandra asked when Judy was going again. David said that he didn't know. She could only visit when her Uncle Ted was free to take her and he hadn't said last time when he'd be able to come again. Sandra was satisfied. It didn't look as if Judy would be able to intrude in David's life very much. She knew Edward Fellowes was a busy man and Sundays were probably the only days he was free. He'd have better things to do than cart his niece around the countryside. She and Joe would have their own car soon and then they'd be able to go on both Saturdays and Sundays. She didn't think that Edward and Rita would intrude if they knew that she and Joe were visiting. They were too well-mannered.

*

David's next letter announced the news.

"The Oaks"

Dear Judy,

I can come home for a few days at Christmas! But the bad news is that I've got to come back here afterwards. They want to go on working on my leg. I suppose that's good because I don't really want to limp for the rest of my life.

Will you bring all your drawings and paintings next time you come, especially the one of "the handsome young man"!

Things are much the same here apart from one thing. Now it's getting cold we don't help in the garden anymore. We do something called Occupational Therapy. There was a choice of things we could do and I've chosen weaving. I'm still learning how to do it but I'll show you what I've done so far when you come.

When can you come again? Your Uncle Ted didn't say when he could bring you next.

David

*

2 Sebastopol Terrace

Dear David,

Yes, that's good news about Christmas but I can't believe you've got to stay on at "The Oaks" after that. Have they any idea at all as to how long you'll have to be there?

But at least now I've got some good news. Auntie Rita told me that she and Uncle Ted used to go walking a lot when they were younger but they'd got out of the habit because they got too busy. She said that the countryside around "The Oaks" is perfect walking country and it reminded them of how much they used to enjoy hiking. They've decided to take up walking again EVERY SUNDAY! They'd be able to drop me off at "The Oaks" and then pick me up at leaving time!

So I'll see you on Sunday and I'll bring the drawings. I can't wait to see your weaving.

Judy

Rita had heard from Judy that David had to stay on at "The Oaks" but could come home for a few days at Christmas. Rita suspected that Sandra would keep Judy away at Christmas while David was at home. He was to be home for less than a week and she knew that Sandra would want to keep him to herself and also keep Judy at bay. But what about what David himself wanted? Was Sandra selfish? Rita came up with a plan.

Sandra came as usual on the Monday morning to help with the administration of Rita's Charity. They were planning some functions in the run up to Christmas and had a lot to get through. Sandra poured out the news about David and was visibly upset. Rita passed her a cup of coffee, commiserated and then announced her plan.

"Well, Sandra, I've been thinking about the terrible time that you and Joe and David have had this year and I have an invitation for you all. You've been through so much that I'd like you to completely relax and spend Christmas Day with us here. We have a traditional Christmas dinner with all the trimmings and it will be an opportunity for you to completely relax. You won't have any cooking to do and you can concentrate on David. If you have Christmas dinner at home I bet you'd spend all morning and half the afternoon in the kitchen and miss out spending time with him. Discuss it with Joe and let me know."

The thought of having Christmas Day in Regent Square was very tempting to Sandra, not to mention the freedom from all the work and the extra time she'd be able to spend with David. How kind

Rita was. Rita had failed to mention that Tim and Judy would be there too. Of course she had. In the glow of Regent Square it didn't even occur to Sandra that Judy would be there. Joe was more than pleased to accept the invitation when Sandra told him that evening and it was agreed that that was how they would spend Christmas Day.

The following Friday, Joe visited Regent Square himself to play his regular game of chess with Edward. After the games Edward brought out the whisky bottle as usual. He asked Joe about David's progress but remembered Rita's advice not to say too much about Judy's visits. It was Joe himself who mentioned Judy.

"It's so kind of you to take Judy to see David, Edward. We appreciate that. It would be too difficult for us to go on both Saturday and Sunday and so it's nice to know that he's got company on some Sundays. I know that Billy Wilson's family always include him in their visit when he doesn't have any visitors himself but it's not the same. And some good news. Mr. Jackson, his tutor, seems to be very pleased with him. He says he's keeping up with what he'd be doing now at Saint Francis."

"That is good news. What's happened to him is bad enough without ending up being behind at school but David's clearly intelligent; he'd have caught up anyway."

Chapter 10

Uncle Patrick, Father Conti, was still mirroring David's situation, neither one being aware of the other's illness or attempted rehabilitation. Patrick had been at the Rest Home for Missionaries far longer than his colleagues had anticipated. Rather than becoming better and stronger, his fevers were recurring and the stomach problems remaining the same. It had been hoped that some rest and treatment would have had him back helping in the Mission much more quickly than it had now turned out. He was clearly not cut out for this work or climate and it was finally agreed that he should be shipped back to England. It would be a long and arduous journey back so the slow progress was arranged in stages with fellow priests meeting him en route and giving him hospitality before sending him on to the next leg of his journey. It was months before he arrived back home and at the docks he was met by an ambulance which took him straight to hospital. All of this had been arranged by Father Anthony at the monastery in Scotland through the network of his Order. He was disappointed and saddened by the knowledge that it was he who was responsible for Patrick's predicament and suffering as it had been his idea, an inspired idea or so he'd thought at the time, to give Patrick a year's break in which to review his life in the Church.

Father Anthony was unable to travel to London himself to visit Patrick and he wondered whether Patrick had informed his family that he was ill and back in England. He knew that he had the details of Patrick's next of kin in his file. Should he write to them or should he ask Patrick if he had done so? If he hadn't, should he himself offer to write to them? He decided to write to Patrick with condolences that the last two, in fact nearly three, years had not worked out as they had hoped and how sorry he was to hear that he was so ill. Had he informed his family? They would probably like to visit him. Would Patrick like him to write to them? Mmmm, thought Father Anthony. He was not at all sure what the future held for Father Conti.

It was at this time and by one of those strange coincidences, or as Judy and David would call it, by telepathy, when Joe suddenly said to Sandra,

"I was working out that it must be going on for about three years since we've heard from Patrick and it's years and years since we've actually seen him."

"Well, he must still be in Africa. I don't suppose it's easy to get post in and out if he's in a remote area."

"Possibly. I wonder how I can find out. Perhaps I could write to the Bishop of the Diocese where he was working before he went to Africa."

"But didn't he go to a monastery in Scotland before he went to Africa?"

"Yes, but I think he'd still be under the jurisdiction of his Bishop."

Sandra didn't want to talk about Patrick. She'd lied to Joe about being Patrick's girlfriend but she supposed that Patrick would never refer to it now that she was married to his brother. Anyway, what did all that matter now? It was years ago.

Sandra changed the subject and asked Joe what he thought a suitable Christmas gift would be for Rita and Edward as a thank you for inviting them for Christmas Day. Joe said that he had no idea and that she was far better at that sort of thing than he was. She then said that they must give David a really big present this year because not only could they now afford it but her poor sweetheart had earned it. They discussed how he'd never complained about the pain he'd been in or about the difficult situation that he was now in. They must think of something that would not only cheer him up but help him in some way.

Joe suggested, "Perhaps it would be better to ask him so that we get him something that he really wants."

"No. A surprise is always best." Sandra responded.

"Only if it's what you want."

Sandra made a further suggestion. "We could get him a new sledge. They're in the shops now."

"But he could only ever use that in the winter and then only if it snowed. I think a new bike's the answer.

He's shot up in height so his old bike's probably too small for him now and cycling will strengthen his legs."

"Yes, that's it, perfect, a new bike!"

Sandra sounded thrilled by the suggestion and Joe, who never won in any discussion with Sandra, had to hide the smile of triumph that had slid, unbidden onto his lips.

*

David couldn't understand why he was feeling so down that morning. Yes, his leg was aching again but that happened most of the time. Why was he different today? He went into the library for his lessons and found Mr. Jackson already there standing at the window with his back to the door. He turned at the sound of the door being closed and wished David good morning. He sensed that something was wrong.

"Is it the pain, David, or something else?"

David was alarmed that this man seemed to know how he felt.

"You and I are in the same boat, David. My leg still hurts sometimes too but when it doesn't hurt isn't it all the sweeter? What I mean is, if we never had pain we wouldn't be aware of how comfortable it is not to be in pain. Have you ever heard of a philosopher called Heraclitus?"

David shook his head.

"Heraclitus said that to get everything you want isn't always a good thing. So, disease makes health seem sweet; when you're hungry you appreciate being fully fed; tiredness creates the enjoyment of resting. You've now learnt through your pain that we cannot know something without the contrast of its opposite. Think about it. Without evil, would we know good? Without war would we know peace? Everything that we think is bad is just a lesson on its opposite."

David followed all this but couldn't help thinking that he'd rather have understood the idea by just being occasionally hungry or tired not learning it through pain. Mr. Jackson wondered if his little homily had hit home or had possibly made things worse. Was bearing pain for a higher ideal what this boy needs to hear at this moment. His own leg was aching too from the shrapnel which was still inside him.

"Wait a moment, David."

He left the room. Ten minutes later he returned with two mugs of hot chocolate and a plate of biscuits.

"Let's remember a time when we were hungry and then we'll enjoy this all the more."

He then dropped his lesson plan and asked David what his plans were for Christmas.

"I can only go home for a few days."

David stopped, then smiled and said,

"But being away from home, not having a home has made me love being at home. I've seen the opposite!"

They both laughed at David's application of Heraclitus' theory. They spent the rest of the morning just talking. Mr. Jackson asked David what he wanted to do when he grew up.

For the first time in his life, David hesitated.

"I've always wanted to be a priest but there are a lot of things that priests can't do and I can't work it out anymore."

David was shocked at his own words. Even he himself hadn't noticed that the build up of unanswered questions had been leading to this admission.

"There's plenty of time to work that out, David." Mr. Jackson said gently.

The dinner bell rang and they stood up to leave. David waited for his homework but Mr. Jackson simply said,

"There are more things in life than learning Latin and Maths. Have a break today."

David wandered into the Occupational Therapy room after dinner and looked at the four small squares that he'd woven so far. He approached the teacher.

"What I'd like to do is a big piece that could hang on the wall like a picture. It's going to be a Christmas present if I can do it."

"Judging from the squares you've done so far I think you could do it so long as you keep it simple. The loom isn't big enough to create what we call a wall-hanging but you could get round that by sewing lots of squares together. You could design each square and choose the colours carefully first on a sheet of paper. When the squares are finished I'll show you how to sew them all together."

He was very keen as he sat down with a sheet of paper, a ruler and some coloured pencils, realising that this was his only hope of giving Judy a Christmas present. He was so lost in his creation that the tea bell startled him. He got up wondering if this was what it was like for Judy when she was drawing and painting. He'd seemed to have gone out of time and place, a place where viruses don't exist, where no shrapnel tears at you, where legs don't ache. He'd discovered another universe; a kind, calm universe; one that he could go to, to ease his pain. He was about to put his work in his drawer when the teacher came back to look at his handiwork.

"Lovely! That's going to be very nice, not too complicated. I'm sure your mother will love it."

He felt a shaft of guilt strike him down. It hadn't even occurred to him to make his mother a present. He knew that his mother loved him. In fact, he knew that she spent every waking hour with him in her thoughts. She'd been devastated when he became ill. How could he not have thought to make a gift for her, or for his father for that matter? He limped down the corridor to the Refectory, the joy of his contemplative afternoon diminishing, fading. Was he a bad person? Was he an ungrateful person? He thought of Mr. Jackson's Heraclitus. What would he say about this? Would he say that now you have witnessed ingratitude you know what gratitude is and appreciate it all the more? How do you know what the light is if you have never seen the darkness?

"David! Come on, quick, there's a birthday cake!"

Little Billy Wilson, as cheerful as ever, broke into David's contemplations, exulting in the party tea laid out on the long table. It was a little boy's birthday and his family had arrived to share the day with him. They were singing "Happy Birthday to you" while the boy smiled and his mother cried.

David smiled as he realised how hungry he was and how feeling hunger now would make the cake taste even sweeter.

*

Sandra was so happy that David was coming home that the mood lightened considerably as she prepared Christmas decorations and thought up menus of David's favourite food. Then, inevitably, or so it seemed to Sandra and Joe, good news was followed by bad. It seemed to them that the proverb was always the wrong way round for them. For them, "Every cloud has a silver lining" had turned out to be "A silver lining always has a cloud wrapped round it." Their latest problem was that despite Joe's promotion, they still couldn't afford a car; they were still relying on the kindness of friends to lend them their cars. There was no station near "The Oaks", nor bus route. Over twenty miles in a taxi was not even worth thinking about. They already knew that the two cars that had been at their disposal would be in use at the time they needed transport. He wouldn't ask Edward if he could borrow his car because although he and Edward had a good, friendly relationship, Joe, like Sandra, was still a little in awe of the Fellowes.

It was Edward himself who solved the problem. News had travelled along the grapevine as usual. David had heard Sandra and Joe discussing the transport problem on their last visit. They hadn't heard him come into the library where he was meeting them and David pretended not to have heard, too surprised and shocked to ask them about it. He told Judy that he may not be able to come home for Christmas after all and reported to her the overheard conversation. Judy told Tim, Tim told Rita, Rita told Edward.

After their last chess game, Edward poured the whisky and he and Joe left the table to settle down into the deep armchairs. Edward had to be careful how he phrased it but as a lawyer he was by nature tactful and discreet.

"So, Joe, I hear you're picking David up next week. Now, I may be jumping the gun here and you might have already organised how you're going to pick him up but Rita and I are going shopping in Westerbridge next week and it occurred to me that "The Oaks" isn't much further on from there. We'd be more than happy to go on and pick David up."

Joe welled up and couldn't speak for a moment.

"Edward, I can't tell you how grateful I am. We didn't know how on earth we were going to pick him up. Thank you so much. That's such a weight off my mind."

"That's settled then."

Edward raised his glass. "To David and his full recovery!"

Sandra was so relieved when Joe gave her the news that she cried again for what could have been the thousandth time that year.

"We'll get through all this, Sandra." Joe put his arms round her and hugged her close.

*

Two days later Rita and Ted were striding across the meadows that lay behind "The Oaks", reinvigorating their spirits that had become bored and jaded as the busy years had passed by. David and Judy watched from the river bank where the frosty morning had left strings of gleaming webs hiding under the bramble bushes. There was a high, pale blue sky, with a flurry of geese flying over, their honking announcing their arrival long before they could be seen. David and Judy suddenly shivered in unison as the sharpness of the air reminded them that it was now winter.

"Can I see your weaving?" asked Judy.

"Have you brought your paintings?"

"No. But there's a reason why I didn't bring them."

"And there's a reason why you can't see my weaving."

They smiled, each knowing what the reason was and looking forward to seeing them at Christmas. David added the news of Christmas Day,

"Mum said yesterday, when she was visiting, that your Auntie Rita's invited Mum and Dad and me to their house for Christmas Day."

"I know. I was so pleased! Dad and I are going too. I didn't think I'd get to see you on Christmas Day."

"Same here."

David moved away the hair that was covering Judy's cheek; the hair that Sandra had called lank and unkempt but which to David's eyes had become a soft, glittering sheet that he kept wanting to make excuses to touch. He felt it in his fingers, then raised it to his lips and kissed it. Judy laughed and kissed his hand. They walked slowly along the river and as David took her hand the luminous time appeared again, the time when the river and its banks, the hedges, the meadows and the trees glowed, the time when the earth illuminates. It was the time of promises, the sign that all will be well. They relaxed into the beauty of their surroundings and the love of their companionship.

It appeared that Rita and Edward had undergone a transformation when they turned up in The Orangery to pick Judy up. They had the fresh pink faces of people who'd been out walking on a frosty day and the exercise had produced in them a sense of relaxed cheerfulness that emanated from them as they sat at the table and described their walk. They promised they'd be back next Sunday as they walked back to the car and then David was alone again. As he walked back up the drive Mr. Jackson, returning from his weekend away, noticed that David looked somewhat morose. He guessed that his visitors had just left and walked alongside him, putting his hand on his shoulder.

"Another favourite philosopher of mine, David, is Epictetus. He's a stoic ...."

*

As the Conti household had begun to settle down again after hearing that David was to stay on at "The Oaks", another shock was about to burst in upon them. The post came early, before Joe went to work and he went to pick up the letter, expecting it to be the usual bill or perhaps even an invitation, but certainly not this mysterious letter which had a postmark on it from a town in Scotland.

"Who do we know in Scotland, Sandra?"

"You'll find out if you open the letter." She snapped.

Joe sighed and finished his breakfast. He'd open it while he was drinking his cup of tea. It lay there in front of him, tempting him to rip it open but for reasons unknown to him he was putting off opening it. He didn't like surprises anymore. He knew it wasn't from Patrick because it wasn't his handwriting. He sipped his tea and then slowly slit the envelope with a knife. He turned the page over to find out who it was from.

"Oh, it's from that monastery that Patrick went to. It's from someone called Father Anthony."

Joe read the letter.

"Oh dear. It appears that Patrick was very ill while he was in Africa and he's now in hospital in London. Good heavens!"

"What's wrong with him?" asked Sandra.

"He has recurrent fevers and some sort of parasite that's upset his digestive system. This Father Anthony says that he's writing to let us know because he thinks that Patrick hasn't been well enough to be in touch with us and he thought that we should know."

"That was thoughtful. Is Patrick in danger? Is that why he's written?"

"He doesn't say. Perhaps I'm supposed to read between the lines. I'd better go and visit him."

"What?" Shrieked Sandra. "You can't just go swanning off to London. It'll be far too expensive and you'd have to stay the night!"

"But he's my brother. I can't just leave him. I'm his only relative now."

Joe and Patrick's parents had married later in life than was usual at that time but had managed to have two children nevertheless. They'd always seemed old to the boys and had died before Joe married but not before seeing Patrick ordained, much to their mother's delight and satisfaction. Joe went to work, deep in thought about what to do about Patrick. Father Anthony had given the name of the hospital and Joe decided that before he did anything else he would phone them. He was glad he had done that before rushing off to London because he was told that Patrick was responding well to treatment but would need to be transferred to a convalescent home for a few weeks rest when he was fully recovered. Joe thought this over. He was about to have both a son and a brother in rehabilitation homes. What was going on? He wondered. Why all at once?

"You're deep in thought, Joe. Good man. Keep it up."

The Managing Director, an elderly man refusing to retire, had walked past Joe's office and mistaken Joe's brooding for intensive calculations on his latest project. When he got home Joe wrote a letter to Father Anthony to thank him for letting him know about Patrick and then set about trying to write to Patrick. He hadn't seen him for so long that he couldn't tune in to the brother he'd shared so much with in the past. He only knew him as the popular, sociable young man he'd gone around with as a teenager and when Patrick was home on holiday from the seminary. He didn't know him as the priest and certainly not as the missionary who'd come home seriously ill. Where to start? He felt hopelessly out of touch and yet wasn't this partly Patrick's fault? He hadn't kept in touch after his Ordination. He came to stay with them only once when he was on leave and hadn't anywhere else to go and that was years ago. He'd write the letter tomorrow.

*

Three loving Sundays passed by with the weekdays in between a frenzy of painting and weaving as David and Judy tried to perfect their gifts for each other. Then, suddenly, or so it seemed, it was time to pick David up for his short home visit. Rita invited Judy to go with them but first they stopped off in Westerbridge to do some shopping. Judy was as entranced with the old city as she had been the first time she went there in the summer but now Christmas lights made it even more enchanting than ever. They returned to the car and drove into the countryside to "The Oaks" where the children were waiting in the library to be picked up. Little Billy Wilson was greeted with ear shattering whoops of joy by his whole family. They were particularly happy because Billy's treatment had finished. He'd be going back to school after the Christmas holidays and seemed to be back to his old self, although his old self had never been far behind. Mr. Jackson was on duty to see that all the children were collected and that their belongings went with them. He and David were alone now and as the old Grandfather clock struck the hour when Rita had said they would come, they heard footsteps in the corridor and Rita, Edward and Judy appeared at the door. David noticed a look of astonishment on Mr. Jackson's face.

"Major Fellowes? Edward? He asked, walking towards them.

"Captain Jackson, Richard!"

The two men clasped each other's hands, exclaiming in surprise at meeting again after so many years and in such unusual circumstances.

Edward had never talked much about his time in the war but Rita had heard enough about his second-in-command, Richard Jackson, to know that here was a man whom her husband had respected and utterly depended upon. In the rare moments when Edward had talked about the horrors that he'd witnessed, the name of Captain Jackson was always at the forefront. Rita, Judy and David stood gaping in amazement at this strange coincidence.

"We lost touch when you were demobbed and went back to London. I wrote to you but everything was still disorganised so I reckoned that the letter never reached you." Edward said.

"I'm afraid my house wasn't there when I got back. The whole street had been wiped out."

"I'm so dreadfully sorry, Richard."

"I did some teaching in London but I couldn't settle to city life and so when I saw the position of tutor advertised for "The Oaks" I jumped at it. I have a little flat up in the attic so it suits me fine."

Edward needed to spend more time with his old comrade but he had to get David home. What could he do? An idea flashed through his mind.

"Christmas. What are you doing at Christmas? Do you have any plans?"

"There's a lovely old pub in the village. They're putting on Christmas dinner so I'll be going there."

"No, Richard. You must come to us for Christmas Day, I insist."

Edward looked over at Rita.

"We've room for one more, haven't we Rita?"

"We certainly have."

"Good heavens, my manners! Richard this is my wife, Rita, and our niece, Judy."

"We really would like you to come to us on Christmas Day", said Rita as she shook hands with the Captain.

"Then, what can I say? I'd love to come." He said.

Judy and David sat in the back of the car, David still reeling from the news that Edward knew his Mr. Jackson. The world seemed to be getting smaller and stranger. Rita and Edward chatted in the front and David felt for Judy's hand and squeezed it. He then stroked her hair lightly with his other hand. The movement attracted Edward's attention and he watched their affection for a moment in the rear view mirror. Their days of playing with toys and making up stories were well and truly over, he thought. Their separation had made them even closer. They certainly weren't drifting apart. They're growing up, he said to himself once again. Then his attention was drawn to Rita's comments about Richard and they enthused again over their chance in a million reunion.

The car stopped outside David's house and Sandra and Joe came running out, full of thanks for Rita and Edward's kindness. David was helped inside even though he was now capable of walking and carrying his case. Tim was waiting for them too when they drove up to Sebastopol Terrace and he invited them to go in and stay for a drink. The conversation was full of Richard Jackson and the machinations of the universe.

Richard Jackson himself went up to his flat up in the attic at "The Oaks" when his duties were over and the Christmas holidays had finally begun. He'd made the little apartment into a comfortable home for himself with lamps, rugs and his favourite Van Gogh print of the Café in Arles. He'd seen many cafés like that when he and Edward were in France. When he'd hung it on the wall he'd wondered why he liked the painting so much when his memories of France were so distressing. He settled down with music on the radio and the newspaper but he couldn't concentrate and dropped the paper onto the floor. He closed his eyes and recalled those days in the war when he and Edward had formed a staunch reliance on each other knowing absolutely that they could depend on each other's knowledge and experience. He hadn't made any friends since then and lived a hermit's life when not on duty. His girlfriend hadn't waited for him to return from the war. Her letters had suddenly stopped and he'd feared the worst, feared for her safety in the bombing of London. When he returned to London he heard that she'd met a GI and had already left for America before Richard himself had even returned. There was no letter, no explanation, just a void where she had been. Perhaps it was time to live in the present, to make a life for himself. Was he still mourning for the lost girl whom he'd hoped to marry when he came back? Was he still mourning for his shattered leg? Was he doing any good here helping the bruised and damaged children who came his way? He thought of David who went some way to making it worthwhile with his quick intelligence and grasp of the opaque mysteries. But a David only came round once in a while. It wasn't enough. His humdrum life was beginning to pall and it was the shock of meeting Edward again that finally made him pull himself out of the pit that he'd dug for himself. He started to look forward to Christmas Day, being sociable again, possibly even enjoying himself.

Chapter 11

David went to his bedroom and stood on the threshold, looking in, as if it was someone else's room and he shouldn't be there. It was the first time he'd been back since that doom-laden day when he'd dragged himself to the lido despite feeling so ill. He remembered little Billy Wilson splashing about and shrieking while Judy bent down to him suggesting that they should go home. He didn't remember much after that apart from waking up in the metal tube. It all seemed such a long time ago. He wandered round the room, picking up things that were where he'd left them and then putting them down again. Something in him seemed to have changed. He couldn't settle. He lay on his bed. Sandra was treating David like an invalid much to Joe's annoyance.

"You must let him do things for himself. He's not ill anymore. You'll actually make him feel ill if you treat him like that."

"We haven't got him here for long. I want him to know how much we love him."

"I don't think he's in any doubt about that. You'll end up making him feel smothered."

Sandra ignored him and continued to wait on David and fuss around him. They'd chosen and bought the bike for David's Christmas present a few weeks previously and it was now residing in the otherwise empty garage. They'd decided to give it to him on Christmas morning after they'd been to Mass and Joe was hoping that David would have time to try it out before going to the Fellowes. Sandra knew that Judy was going to Midnight Mass with the older members of the Wilson family so there'd be no chance of her holding them up after Mass or David asking if she could go home with them for breakfast. She was hoping for a completely Judy-free Christmas.

Joe was in his study trying again to write a letter to Patrick. He wouldn't catch the last post before Christmas if he didn't do it now. Then he realised that all he needed to do was to send Patrick a Christmas card. He would write in the card that he hoped that Patrick was recovering and that he would write to him in the New Year. He did it at once, walked straight to the pillar box and came home in a much better frame of mind and mood. He chatted to Sandra about how he was looking forward to seeing David's face when they uncovered the bike. She put her finger to her lips and warned him that David might hear and that would spoil the surprise. They looked at each other, listening for any sign of David and then they both giggled quietly like a couple of children.

*

After Rita and Edward had left Sebastopol Terrace it occurred to Tim that he still didn't know how Judy was feeling about the discovery that Auntie Marie was her mother. She'd certainly been quieter than usual but then she'd been studying for the end of term exams and working furiously on finishing her art projects. Had she given up her desire to write to her mother and even to want to see her? At dinner that evening, he broached the subject again but Judy just said that there was obviously no way of getting in touch with her mother if it would upset her so much, according to what Tim had told her. He apologised again for keeping the truth from her for so long. Judy looked into Tim's worried face. She felt a wave of pity for his discomfort but it was his fault after all. Hadn't he kept the knowledge of her mother from her, hadn't he prevented her from getting in touch with or meeting her mother?

"It was just such a shock, Dad, and knowing that you'd known the truth all the time." Said Judy at last.

Tim acknowledged that that was true and he apologised yet again. But Judy had plans; the possibility of a new course of action had occurred to her and she would pursue it. There was no need for Tim to know about it.

Christmas Day finally dawned. After Mass Sandra and Joe took David into the garage and unveiled the bike. They'd have liked a trumpet fanfare but the look on his face was reward enough.

He climbed on and rode down the drive easily and then back up to where they were standing. He started back down the drive and called,

"I'll do a circuit round the estate."

"No, have your breakfast first."

*

Rita's Christmas Days always followed the same routine. From eleven o'clock to one o'clock there was Open House with drinks and canapés for relatives, friends, colleagues, neighbours and anyone she'd taken a shine to during the year. This year she had invited an up and coming artist named Jane Stevens whom she'd met at the Viridian Gallery in Westerbridge. Rita had bought two of her paintings and by chance, Jane was there at the time delivering more of her work for an exhibition. Rita had sent an invitation care of the gallery, not knowing that Jane lived locally. The drawing room at Regent Square oozed festive splendour with a huge tree standing at one of the floor to ceiling windows. Long branches of holly lay along the length of the marble mantelpiece while ivy dripped from each corner. Red candles in glimmering brass candlesticks stood on the long table against the far wall where the canapés had been set out. A separate table held the drinks and glasses. All was tasteful, not a bauble or strip of tinsel to be seen. Judy was offering the trays and plates to the guests, wearing a little frilly apron, exactly like the ones she'd admired on the waitresses when she and Rita had visited the new Department Store Restaurant. Edward was on duty at the drinks table. Rita floated amongst her guests as the hostess. She was aware that the artist, Jane Stevens, might not know any of the guests so she went over to talk to her and decide who she should introduce her to. While they were talking, Jane noticed the new girl from her class carrying plates, the orphaned girl who Jane had regretted asking about her background. My goodness, she thought, is she working? Is she having to earn a few pence at the weekends? Surely she's too young? Rita noticed a look of consternation on Jane's face and asked her if everything was alright.

"I've just noticed one of my pupils, the girl there in the little apron. I'm teaching part-time at Saint Catherine's and that girl's in one of my classes. In fact she's my star pupil, very talented."

"That girl, Jane, is Judy, my niece." Smiled Rita.

Jane Stevens was so taken aback that she couldn't reply. She remembered her conversation with Judy, how she'd pitied this little orphan, regretted asking her about her background and now she turns out to be related to the owners of a house in Regent Square.

"I didn't know you were at Saint Catherine's, Jane. I'm so pleased to hear that Judy's talented but I've already seen some of her work and I must say I was impressed. I'm not surprised though now I know who her teacher is."

Jane took the compliment graciously and said nothing about her conversation with Judy, hoping that Judy, in her turn, had said nothing about the new intrusive teacher. When Rita discovered that Jane Stevens lived alone and would not be bothering to make herself a Christmas dinner, Rita insisted that she should come back later in the afternoon and join them again for dinner.

Sandra, Joe and David were also due to arrive later in the afternoon for the early evening Christmas dinner so in the meantime Edward and Richard went into the study to have their long awaited catch-up, Rita went to lie down and a team from a local restaurant worked in the Fellowes' kitchen to create the perfect Christmas dinner. Tim and Judy strolled back home, along the fine Georgian streets to the brook, past the bandstand and home through Alma Park. As they approached, they noticed a young man on a bike waiting outside their house.

"David!" called Judy, running to meet him.

"We've got a couple of hours before we go to your Auntie's. Shall we go for a walk or are you busy? Hello, Mr. Forrester, happy Christmas."

"Happy Christmas, David." Tim had caught up with them. "How are you? I haven't seen you for such a long time but Judy's been keeping me up to date with how you're getting on."

"I'm a lot better, thank you. I have to go back "The Oaks" after Christmas but I don't think it'll be for long."

"That's good. I hear you'll be joining us at Rita's this afternoon."

"Yes, but have Judy and I got time for a walk? Is that alright?"

"Yes, but don't be late back, Judy."

They walked away, David wheeling his new bike alongside Judy and bending down to talk to her. Tim watched them and then went inside the house alone. He thought about going next door to wish Nora a happy Christmas but remembered that she was going to spend the day at Inkerman Terrace with her son's family. He'd seen her last night when she brought Judy back from midnight mass and they'd exchanged their Christmas pleasantries then. He put on some music and dozed.

*

At half-past three the group re-gathered. Sandra was surprised to see other guests. She'd been under the impression that they had been especially invited to share Christmas with Rita and Edward. She was even more surprised to see Mr. Jackson, David's tutor and who was that woman looking like a pre-Raphaelite model? Soon, everyone was introduced and all was made clear. She was just thinking that at least the Forresters weren't there when Tim and Judy arrived. Judy was wearing a dress that Rita had obviously chosen for her and Sandra noticed that she was now wearing stockings and not socks. That's far too young, she thought, and the delight at coming to Rita's for an enjoyable, quiet dinner faded.

At the beginning of the meal Edward raised his glass to Sandra, Joe and David and wished them a New Year and new decade that would bring an end to the trials of the Conti family. Jane Stevens suddenly said,

"Conti? Is that your name? I knew a priest once called Conti. It's an unusual name; could he be a relative of yours? Patrick Conti?"

"Yes, that's my brother." Laughed Joe.

Before he could ask how Jane knew him, Sandra cut in,

"How do you know Patrick?" She asked in a brittle, almost challenging voice.

Jane had been enjoying the wine and was oblivious to the tone.

"I used to go to his youth club when I was a teenager. He was so popular, all the girls were in love with him, and he was so good-looking but that's obviously a family trait." She said grinning at Joe and David.

Sandra was outraged. This tipsy woman was complimenting a married man in public and in front of his wife. She looked at Joe for confirmation of her feelings but he and David were smiling, delighted by the compliment.

Jane carried on in full flood,

"The girls used to say what a waste that he was a priest because priests can't get married." She laughed at the memory of it.

David glanced at Judy. Jane hadn't finished.

"Now that I've seen David in the flesh I can see how well you caught him in your drawing, Judy."

"Drawing? What drawing?" Snapped Sandra.

"Judy did a very good charcoal sketch of David from her photo of him."

"Photo? What photo? Snapped Sandra again, two red patches appearing on her cheeks. She was furious. That girl taking photos of her son, without Sandra being told about them or even shown them. And taking them in to school. Whatever next?

Sandra glared at Judy.

"Why haven't I seen any of these?" She demanded.

But suddenly becoming aware of how aggressive she was beginning to sound, she softened her tone and giving Judy one of her special smiles said,

"I'd love to see your photos and pictures of David."

"I would have shown them to you but I haven't seen you for such a long time." Judy responded.

Sandra knew exactly why she hadn't seen Judy for such a long time. Hadn't it been her own idea to keep her at bay? Now as a result of that things were going on behind her back. Jane continued, happily unaware of the rumpus she was causing.

"We loved that Youth Club and then Father Conti suddenly disappeared. We couldn't understand it and when someone else came in to run it, it wasn't the same at all so it just sort of disintegrated and closed. So perhaps you can solve the mystery, Joe. Why did he suddenly leave and where did he go?"

"To be honest, Jane, Patrick didn't keep in touch very well and we heard from him briefly that he'd gone to a monastery in Scotland."

Before he could go on, Jane yelped,

"A monastery! Father Conti! That doesn't sound like him!"

"When you're a priest you go where your Bishop sends you. From there he went to the Missions in Africa." Sandra explained in a supercilious tone.

"Well, I never." Jane responded.

"Actually, it's interesting that you've brought him up. We've just heard recently that he'd been very ill in Africa and he's been sent back. We're waiting to hear how he is." Joe added.

"Oh Joe, I'm so sorry to hear that." Said Rita. "After all that's happened to David and now your own brother too. There's no end to it, although I must say that David's looking very well."

They all looked at David and he smiled a sheepish grin. Sandra was not to be outdone.

"Speaking of Patrick, there's a tradition in Joe's family. They have a chalice that goes back centuries. The eldest son of each generation always becomes a priest and the chalice is handed down to him at his Ordination."

She said this looking at David.

Richard Jackson, who had been sitting quietly through the various conversations said,

"What if the eldest son doesn't want to be a priest?"

Sandra was affronted.

"That's never happened. The eldest sons have always been blessed with a vocation. It's as if they are born with it."

David looked uncomfortable and glanced at Judy again.

Edward felt discomfort in the room and suggested that they should retire to the more comfortable surroundings of the Drawing Room for their coffee. Rita was relieved and went into the kitchen to tell the team. During the to and fro David and Judy managed to slip out. They took their coats off the stand, took the key off the peg that opened the gate to the little copse in the middle of the Square and escaped into the summer house.

"My mother's watching me like a hawk. She won't let me do anything because she thinks I'm still ill. Tomorrow, I'll say I want to go for a ride on my bike and it'll be good for my leg. That might do it. I'll see if I can come over tomorrow."

They were sitting in the summer house, unwrapping the gifts they'd made for each other when they heard an anguished cry.

"David, where are you?"

The other guests knew that as the only children in the group David and Judy would not have wanted to sit while the adults sipped their brandy and chatted but Sandra wouldn't settle until the house had been searched for David. When she heard that he must be outside she was horrified.

"If he catches a chill after all he's been through, I don't know what will happen to him."

As they passed under the mistletoe that was dangling from the chandelier in the hall David bent down and kissed Judy on her forehead. At that moment, Jane Stevens walked past them on the way to the bathroom. She was tempted to say,

"You won't be able to do that when you're a priest!"

But she didn't.

Chapter 12

1960

The nineteen- sixties roared across the country on January 1st and brought a blast of fresh air with it. The nineteen- fifties dropped off the edge into oblivion. Judy had one resolution and one resolution only and that was to track down her own family. She was banned from getting in touch with her mother so she would find her father, using the bits of information that Tim had given her. As soon as the local library opened after the holidays she walked up to the librarian who she knew had worked there for a long time. Judy was well known at the library.

"Good morning, Judy and happy New Year!"

"Hello Mrs. Nicholson", Judy said, "Happy New Year."

"And what are you looking for today?"

Judy decided not to launch immediately into her real reason for speaking to Mrs. Nicholson and said that she'd like a book on the history of art.

"Come on, I'll show you what we've got."

The library was empty and Judy took the opportunity while they were standing in front of the art books.

"Do you remember my Auntie Marie, who used to work here?"

"Oh yes, of course I do, although it was quite a long time ago. I've noticed a family resemblance; you look like her, especially as you've got older."

"Really? I've never met her, except when I was a baby but of course I don't remember."

"It was a pity that she had to go and look after her cousin. I think that was it – her cousin was very ill and had no-one to help her so your auntie left her job and her home just like that to help her. Such a kind girl."

Yes, that was the story that had been put about, thought Judy, so she'd better be careful. Then, as casually as she could, Judy asked the next question.

"Dad and I were talking about her the other day and he said she'd had a boyfriend, a Freddie somebody?"

"Ooh yes, Freddie Alexander. He's a descendant of Sir William, you know, the one who used to live at "The Oaks" - that big house that's a school now."

Judy's heart missed a beat. Was she a descendant of Sir William? Was this Freddie her father? Had her forebears owned the mansion that was now David's school?

Fortunately for Judy the librarian was keen on local history and talked about the history of the Alexander family.

"Sir William used "The Oaks" as a kind of retreat at weekends and holiday times but during the week he lived in his town house in Regent Square."

"Really? Said Judy, again, becoming increasingly astonished with each revelation. "My auntie and uncle live there."

"They'll probably know the Alexanders then because the family still lives there. "The Oaks" was sold a long time ago but they retained the town house and it's been handed down through the years. The same family still lives there after all these generations. Fascinating."

"Does Freddie still live there?"

"I don't know. He'll be in his thirties by now, I imagine. He owns an art gallery in Westerbridge, The Viridian Gallery, I think it's called."

Judy was speechless at this flow of coincidences. She was excited at the thought of being an Alexander but then the sadness of having been abandoned returned. A customer was standing at the desk and Mrs. Nicholson said that she must go.

Judy went home and wrote David a manic letter, telling him the news and declaring that she would go to the art gallery and face Freddie Alexander. She was being prevented from seeing her mother but it now looked as if she could get in touch with her father. David wrote by return of post begging her not to confront a stranger claiming to be his daughter. She must think of a more subtle way of finding out. She mustn't forget that Marie had told Tim that she hadn't told the father that she was having a baby.

Tim and Judy were at Rita's for Sunday lunch. When Rita and Judy were alone and Tim was out of earshot, Judy asked Rita if she knew the Alexanders.

"Yes, they live directly opposite here on the other side of the copse. Why do you ask?"

"Did you know they were related to Sir William Alexander?"

"Not at first, but we met them at a party and someone mentioned it. They talked a bit about the history of the family in Victorian times and the impact on this area. That's when Uncle Ted got interested and read Sir William's biography and took the opportunity to have a good look round "The Oaks" on one of our visits there, do you remember?"

"Have you ever met their son, Freddie?"

"Yes, he's the owner of the gallery in Westerbridge where I first met Jane Stevens. Why all these questions about the Alexanders all of a sudden?"

"Freddie Alexander was Auntie Marie's boyfriend, or should I say, my mother's boyfriend?"

Rita put her hand to her mouth and looked horrified.

"What? Are you sure? How could you know? We never met her boyfriend."

Rita sat still staring into the garden and then continued in a quiet voice, almost talking to herself.

"But he *was* called Freddie. I do remember that. But there must be quite a few other Freddies around. Why would you suppose it was that particular Freddie?"

Judy didn't explain how she knew.

"Does he live with his parents, here, in Regent Square?"

"No, he lives in Westerbridge."

"What's he like?"

"Judy, I think I know where this is going. No-one knows who your father is and Marie absolutely refused to name him."

"But she only had one boyfriend and she was only seventeen. How could it be anyone else? He must have deserted her when he found out she was having a baby."

"We just don't know, Judy, which is why we can't accuse anyone. And she told Tim that she hadn't told the father that she was having a baby."

"We don't know that for sure. There've been so many lies, how can we know what's true?"

Rita felt sick. What was Judy going to do? She was self-willed and fearless. Would she go and speak to him, perhaps ask him outright if he was her father? Rita squirmed at the thought. She decided that perhaps she should have a quiet word with him. But what could she say? It was just too awkward and embarrassing. How could she bring the conversation round to Marie and even if she managed it how could she bring it round to the question?

"You're both deep in thought." Said Ted as he came into the room. "What devious plans are afoot?" He said in a mock accusatory voice.

He couldn't have been nearer the truth.

Tim came back into the room and after some discussion as to how to spend the afternoon, the four of them decided to go for a stroll. Nothing more could be said as neither Rita nor Judy wanted Tim to find out what was going on. Rita decided to tell Ted later and see what he thought. Judy would be back at school in a few days time and that might take her mind off it. Then she had a thought and caught up with Ted, leaving Judy a bit behind with Tim.

"Ted, the weather's not too bad for January. Shall we go walking on Sunday and drop Judy off at "The Oaks"?

The time after Christmas and New Year always hung heavy and Ted brightened at the thought of a long, brisk walk in that rolling countryside.

"Judy, are you free next Sunday? Shall we drop you off at "The Oaks"?

The suggestion had the same effect on Judy as the thought of a walk had had on Ted. She brightened immediately and thanked them, happy at the thought of seeing David again.

*

David also had something on his mind when they met on Sunday. The weather was sharp but dry so they walked by the river.

"Mum's been worried that since I've been here I haven't had any Religious instruction and haven't had the chance to go to Mass so she asked Father O'Brien about it. He got in touch with the local priest and he's going to come every week for an hour. I was hoping that Matron would say that it wasn't possible but she seemed glad about it."

"But why don't you want it? If you're going to be a priest you'll have to keep up with the study."

"That's just it, though. Father O'Brien told this priest that I've got a vocation so he's talking about it all the time but I really want to think it through for myself. I want all these people to stop going on about it. Do you remember when you said that perhaps we don't have vocations? That we are free to choose for ourselves? I've been feeling like that lately. I want to disentangle it all and find out."

Judy was worried that what she'd said might deter David from the priesthood. What if God really was calling David to be a priest and she had suggested that this might not be so? She feared that if that was so she would be guilty of a grievous sin and condemned. She tried to explain her fear to David but he just said,

"I've decided that God's not like that. They tell us that God throws us into Hell for all sorts of things and then in the next breath they say he's all merciful."

"But they also say that he's all just."

"What's *just* about sending someone to Hell forever and ever just because they make a suggestion that the Church might be wrong?"

They sat in gloomy silence with the fires of Hell raging at their feet, both afraid. After a while, David looked up, spread out his arms and changed the subject.

"Just think, if Freddie Alexander really is your father, this is where your ancestors lived!"

"I don't know how to ask him. Auntie Rita says we have no proof and so I can't do it. She knows him really well and it would be embarrassing."

"Could you tell him that you've just found out that Marie's your mother and as you can't remember her you're trying to build up a picture of her and so you're sort of interviewing anyone who knew her?"

Judy grabbed David's arm,

"Oh, David, that's brilliant!"

She kissed his hand and as the wind blew her hair across her face he gently brushed it back. They were startled when the tea bell rang. They were aware that the shrill sound had broken a spell, a spell which as yet they couldn't identify. They walked up to the Orangery where they were met by Rita and Ted, glowing from their walk.

In the car going home, Judy was very quiet. Rita wondered if Judy had any plans regarding Freddie Alexander but decided not to ask. She'd talked to Ted about it and he felt that Judy was treading on dangerous ground and should be warned not to approach him. The three sat in the car with their own silent thoughts.

The following Friday, after school, Judy decided to go straight to the station. She knew where The Viridian Gallery was in Westerbridge because she'd been in that area with Rita before they'd picked David up for the Christmas holidays. A terrific snowstorm had just started when she got off the train and by the time she arrived at the gallery she was drenched, her long hair bedraggled, her shoes squelching. The neatly black-suited receptionist was not pleased to see this teenager, as Judy now appeared to be, soaking wet and rough-looking, abusing this cultured art space. Did she think she could use the gallery to shelter from the snow? Was she going to wander around until the snow stopped, pretending that she could buy any of this artwork? Or was she looking for something to pilfer; she looked like one of those gypsy girls from The Common. But Judy spoke first.

"Could I speak to Mr. Freddie Alexander, please?"

The receptionist was taken aback. What possible reason could this girl have for speaking to the owner of an Art Gallery?

"He's extremely busy and you can only see Mr. Alexander if you have an appointment."

The receptionist continued with her work, then looked up at Judy with distaste, waiting for her to leave. At that moment, the office door opened and Rita and Freddie emerged.

"Judy, my goodness, what are you doing here? Freddie, this is my niece, Judy."

The receptionist stood up quickly nearly knocking her chair over,

"Oh, I'm sorry! I didn't know, I ………"

No-one heard her as the introductions took place.

"You're absolutely soaking, Judy."

Freddie looked at the receptionist.

"Please could you bring Judy a hot drink? Tea or coffee, Judy?"

"Thank you. Tea, please."

"And biscuits", Freddie called after the retreating figure.

"It's alright, Freddie, I can take Judy straight home."

Rita was desperate to get Judy away from Freddie but he insisted that she should take off her wet coat and have a drink.

"Could I speak to you for a moment, if you have the time?" Judy asked.

"Yes, of course. Fire away." Freddie replied.

"In private."

"Judy!" Rita said quickly. "I really think we'd better get home."

"It's ok, Auntie Rita, I've got a return ticket and a timetable so if you're in hurry I'll be ok getting home."

"I've got the car and the snow's stopped. We'll get home much quicker than the train."

"Ok, thank you. The car will be nicer, but could you wait a few minutes until I've spoken to Mr. Alexander?"

Rita gave up. She'd tried her best. Judy and Freddie went into his office and Rita waited for the storm to break.

"So, Judy, how can I help you?"

Judy followed the plan that David had suggested. She was "interviewing" people who'd known her mother. Freddie was bemused by the information that Marie was Judy's mother. How could she be? He'd heard that she'd become a nun after helping her cousin who was ill. Judy decided to tell him the whole story, that is, the truth. He gasped with shock and poured out a flow of questions, to himself, rather than to Judy.

"So when she told me that she was going to look after a relative, she was actually having a baby? I don't understand. But who could the father have been? She wasn't the sort of girl to have more than one boyfriend at a time. I really don't understand. So who on earth was the father and how on earth could that have happened? As far as I knew she was only seeing me and I know for definite that I couldn't be the father."

He looked embarrassed at this point, having to say such things to a young girl. But Judy felt that her unasked question had been answered. He'd seemed genuinely shocked. She believed him.

"I'm sorry I've given you a shock, Mr. Alexander. Please can we keep Marie's secret? No-one knows the truth apart from the family. Auntie Rita had warned me not to talk to you about this so please don't blame her."

He appeared dazed.

"Of course not. I'm glad that I know. I never understood why she finished with me. Going to help a relative wouldn't have been a problem. I even told her that I could borrow my father's car and we could still see each other. But she was adamant that she didn't want to see me again. To be honest, I was hurt. We seemed to be getting on so well. Oh well, at least I know now."

Rita, who had been waiting to hear a burst of outrage, was intrigued that all had remained quiet. They came out of the office. He shook Judy's hand.

"Thank you for coming, Judy."

Rita was very keen to hear the outcome of the conversation but intuitively didn't ask.

"It's ok, Auntie Rita, he's not my father."

"Did you actually ask him if he was?"

"No, it was obvious from what he said."

Rita was intrigued to know how the conversation had gone but she decided not to pry as she felt certain that Freddie would tell her.

As soon as she got home, Judy wrote to David.

2 Sebastopol Terrace

Dear David,

My ancestors didn't dance in the ballroom at "The Oaks" or wait for their carriage in Regent Square. Freddie Alexander isn't my father. I went to see him at his gallery and I was very careful, like you suggested, but it's clear that he didn't know what was going on with Marie. There are no more clues. He was the only boyfriend she ever had. I wish I hadn't started thinking about who my parents are. It's driving me crazy.

I'm lying on my bed looking at the wall hanging you wove. It's beautiful, just like the sun setting over our river. Just think, if you hadn't had to go to "The Oaks", Uncle Ted would never have met up with his old army friend. Odd, isn't it?

Judy

"The Oaks"

Dear Judy,

I'm surprised that Freddie isn't your Dad, especially as your Miss Stevens had suggested that art might run in the family. He would have been the obvious one, the right name too. The only one who knows the truth is Marie so you'll have to somehow get in touch and make her tell you. We'll talk about it on Sunday.

David

Chapter 13

As Judy and David sank into gloom and wrestled with their problems, their angst was mirrored again by Patrick, Father Conti, who was now back at the monastery in Scotland. He was recovering well physically but spiritually and emotionally, not so well. He was now back to reflecting on what he should do in the future when he was completely better and would have to return to his work. But what was his work? He asked himself. If he was to remain a priest, what was he to do, as the thought of returning to a parish made his heart sink? Should he stay in the monastery, if they would have him, become a monk and spend the rest of his days in silence? The little worm that had crawled into his brain once before paid a return visit. He could give the whole lot up. He could go out into the world a free man and do whatever he wanted. His heart reacted to the thought sending an excitement through him that the other choices hadn't created. He would work with young people but not under the command of a Bishop who had no understanding of what he was trying to do. He would have to do it as a lay person, not a priest. But, he realised with a jolt that he would still have the powers of the priesthood. He'd been anointed in which case no-one could take away his God-given power. He would be as successful as he had been previously. His schemes for young people would be ground-breaking; their popularity would spread throughout the whole country. This was not pride, of course, he would simply be using his God-given gifts. He was sure now that he must leave the priesthood. He would inform the ever-patient Father Anthony the very next day.

He'd received the Christmas card from Joe and the subsequent letter. He was shocked to hear that his nephew had had polio. He could have died, Patrick thought, and then what would have happened to the Conti dynasty? He couldn't remember much about David. Was he about thirteen now? Was he being groomed to be the next receiver of the chalice? He wondered how his relatives would take his news that he was to leave the priesthood. He was excited about his decision but then an anxiety started to lay hold of him. Could you take back promises that you've made to God? Betraying your king required a death sentence. What of betrayal of God? Anxiety turned to fear and fear into heavy-footed dread.

The next day Father Anthony was distressed to see that Patrick had once again been attacked by the recurrent fever that had so debilitated him. He was on fire, raging and delirious, apparently at the Gates of Hell. An ambulance was called and Patrick was once again taken to hospital. Father Anthony decided to write to Patrick's brother for a second time. The illness was serious; he didn't know where it would lead. The family must be told. So, having persuaded himself that it was the right thing to do, Father

Anthony wrote another letter to Joe. He knew from Patrick that his brother's child had been dangerously ill and he was loath to add to their misery but what could he do?

Joe picked up the letter with the Scottish postmark and sighed. Going to the north of Scotland was out of the question. The same question was heard: but what can I do?

*

There was a buzz at "The Oaks" when Judy arrived. Visitors and staff were in groups discussing something obviously important but Judy and David set off for the river.

"They're talking about this place closing down." David reported. "They say it's going to be sold and they'll use the money to build a better, more modern place nearer to Westerbridge."

"I wonder who would have enough money to buy a place like this."

"I heard someone say that it'll probably be pulled down and they'll build houses here."

"But there's some even bigger news, two lots of big news, no three!"

Judy stopped, waiting for the news.

"I can leave at Easter. They've done all they can for my leg."

"What does that mean? Does it mean it's better or they've given up?"

"They say that if I do a lot of sport or walking it might ache afterwards but it's a lot stronger now and they think it'll be ok."

"But that's brilliant! You're coming home; you'll be able to start at Saint Francis! We can do all the things again that we used to do! These few months will be just like a bad dream, a nightmare that you once had and it'll fade just like dreams do."

His eyes filled with tears and he turned away so that she wouldn't see. She took his hand and said that they knew that all would be well. They sat in silence holding hands until Judy said,

"That's two pieces of news, what's the third, I hope it's good news."

"It's the best news ever." David cheered up. "Mr.Jackson's got a job at Saint Francis'. He'll be my Latin and English teacher. He said that when he goes to see your Uncle Ted, Miss Stevens, your Art teacher's often there and she told him about the post. So going to my new school won't be so bad. I was bothered about starting a new school when the rest of the boys had already been there for two terms. But some of them were at our old school so I'll know some of them and now Mr.Jackson will be there too."

Talking about it made the nervousness creep back and he changed the subject.

"It's a pity that Freddie Alexander isn't your Dad. He could have sold all your paintings and let you work in his gallery."

"He doesn't have to be my Dad to do that – he could do that anyway if I was good enough. The main point is that I still don't know who my Dad is but there's someone who does know and they won't tell. It's maddening."

"We'll be thirteen soon. Teenagers!" David said.

"In some places, being thirteen's special. It's like the gateway to adulthood." Said Judy with a dreamy look, "I can't wait to be grown up."

"Romeo and Juliet were only fourteen, did you know?" David asked.

The sharp tea bell cut through the question and that indefinable spell was broken again. Now, very quiet, they walked to the Orangery, still holding hands.

*

The following week, Freddie Alexander, Jane Stevens, Rita and Edward sat in the drawing room in Regent Square discussing the future of "The Oaks".

They were determined that the county should not lose that architectural gem, nor the beautiful gardens and setting. They all agreed that the lack of a station or bus route would be an obstacle to the place becoming an Arts Centre holding concerts, films, and exhibitions which is what they would have all liked. It would have been the perfect venue but unrealistic. The huge cost of buying and restoring the place was the biggest drawback although there were grants to be had, the council might like a share, individuals and companies might like to be part of it, whatever "it" ended up being. It was not dissimilar to the rescue of the lido although on a much bigger scale.

Jane came up with a plan that the house could be turned into a series of working studios, some for artists, some for sculptors and so on. There was certainly enough space for large studios and also enough space for small apartments so that the artists could live and work on site. Freddie felt that art was a precarious business and artists may not be able to afford such a place. And so they chattered on, excited by their new venture until it was time for dinner.

Richard Jackson had also been invited to dinner and he arrived in time to hear their latest ideas and feel their mixture of excitement and despondency. He'd been living up to his promise to himself that he would start living again; try to be in the present and leave the horrors behind. He was fascinated by Jane Stevens. He'd never met anyone before who was so bold in her behaviour. She would say what she thought, regardless of the company present, passionately passing on her thoughts on any variety of subjects. He'd observed, in his quiet way, how she'd upset Sandra Conti at the Christmas dinner. There'd been the mention of Joe's brother, the priest, which had upset her for some reason which he couldn't fathom and then there was the compliment she'd given to Sandra's husband and son which Sandra had clearly disliked. He recalled that Sandra had told the story of the family's chalice that passed through the generations of Conti priests. He was also aware of her intense devotion to David which almost bordered on hysteria. This was understandable when he was seriously ill but surely not so necessary now? He feared for David and the chalice. He was brought out of his reverie by Jane regaling them with stories of the shenanigans at St. Francis' and St. Catherine's.

On first meeting Jane, Sandra had thought of her as looking like a pre-Raphaelite model, the word "bohemian" coming into her mind but not in a complimentary way. Richard had thought the same but with a feeling quite the opposite to Sandra's. He was a quiet, thoughtful man. Living in his little attic at "The Oaks" alone during the evenings and weekends, mixing only with children and a few teachers and nurses during the day had increased his quietness and detachment from the world. It had suited him to bury himself away from a world so full of harshness and misery. After meeting Edward again, his world had suddenly opened up and gradually he'd realised that he was ready to give up his hermitage. When he first met Jane at Christmas, just a few days after meeting Edward, he wasn't yet ready for the full force of her vivacity. In fact it had first of all sent him into a state of silent shock, making him feel out of his depth. They started to meet regularly at Rita and Edward's and every time he was invited to Regent Square he realised that he was hoping that she would be there, looking forward to seeing her again.

They continued discussing the future of "The Oaks" over dinner. It was decided that they would hold an open public meeting in Westerbridge but also personally invite the Council, organisations and companies who might be interested. They agreed on a date and Rita would book a hall, send out the invitations and place notices in the local papers inviting anyone interested to come to the meeting. They were satisfied with their efforts and left feeling more cheerful. Richard offered Jane a lift home and on the way, he mentioned a new play that he was hoping to see. Would she like to go too, he would get the tickets? He'd been planning something like this for quite a while but always backed out, feeling sure that she would not want someone like him as a companion, although he admitted to himself that he wanted more than just her companionship. He was relieved and not a little surprised when she accepted in her cheerful, energetic way. That play was the beginning of more plays, films, exhibitions and then cosy meals out. When Richard relocated to teach at St. Francis' he'd be a lot nearer and perhaps they could do even more together, not just be reliant on his alternate free Saturdays.

Chapter 14

The day that David came home for good was a day long awaited by those who loved him. Edward had offered to collect him as he had done at Christmas and although Sandra would have liked to have gone too she was reluctant to ask, still being in awe of the Fellowes. "The Oaks" was forlorn, packing up and ready to close. Richard greeted them in the library as on the momentous occasion at Christmas. He was to dine with them on Easter Saturday evening and there was an air of celebration, caused not only by David's recovery and homecoming but by Richard's relocation to their neighbourhood. One of those delightful coincidences had happened just after Richard's successful application to teach at St. Francis'. Nora Wilson had been invited by her son and daughter-in-law to live with them in their house in Inkerman Terrace. They had one of the huge Victorian villas and Nora would have her own bedroom and sitting room. She helped out a lot so it made sense for them all to live together as she had told Tim when she went round to give him the news.

Tim knew from Edward that his friend, Richard, would be moving to the area and he told him that Nora's house would be going up for sale. Richard had spent only a fraction of his money while living at "The Oaks" and after a discussion with Nora discovered that he could afford her cottage. It wasn't even put up for sale and Richard moved in on Maundy Thursday. Jane spent Good Friday helping Richard to unpack and decide where to put his meagre belongings. It came as a shock when Jane opened a box to find one of her own paintings inside. Richard looked sheepish and said that he'd been admiring her paintings from even before he'd got to know her. After Easter they were going to Westerbridge to choose furniture as Richard had none at all. He was to stay with Edward and Rita until he had at least a bed, a table and a chair. It was quite a celebration on Easter Saturday at Rita's. Along with Jane and Richard she'd invited Tim and Judy and Freddie Alexander. Freddie winked at Judy, implying that her secret conversation with him was safe.

After everyone had left and Richard was seeing Jane home before returning for the night, Rita asked Edward if he thought that Jane and Richard were getting rather friendly. She'd paused before the word "friendly" as if searching for a better word.

"They're like chalk and cheese." He commented. "Exact opposites. There's that saying though that opposites attract and that certainly seems to be the case. I think you're right. There's definitely something going on there. I hope so, anyway. Richard could certainly do with a break."

Richard and Jane's friendship had progressed quickly into a strong mutual attraction. They'd kept their liaison discreet and presumed that no-one knew how much time they were spending together. That was odd considering how obvious it had been to everyone else. Tim was pleased that the transaction for Nora's house had gone through so easily and he called in to welcome Richard to Sebastopol Terrace. He discovered that Judy's art teacher was there helping. He invited them to come next door for a cup of tea when they'd finished. Judy was upstairs drawing and she rushed down when she heard the voices. She had some, but only a few, favourite people, and here was one and possibly two of them. She wondered if Mr. Jackson and Miss Stevens were going out together. She must tell David. She wouldn't be able to see him until after Easter Monday because Sandra had all kinds of activities lined up for them while Joe was on holiday from work. She was going to fully enjoy David's return and enfold him back into the nest. David had to re-orientate himself back into what his life had been before his illness. Everything seemed the same but on another level everything was different.

*

Fortunately for Father Conti the gates of Hell had remained closed. For the time being. As the fever abated the delirium receded and he was once more back at the monastery. Father Anthony asked him what he would like to do. Should he get in touch with his Bishop and arrange for his return to his parish? Then the decision seemed clear to Patrick.

"No, Father, I've decided to leave the priesthood but I don't know how. I've promised, I've taken vows. How can I undo a vow?"

The decision was not a shock to Father Anthony. He'd thought for some time that this would be how the whole saga would end. He asked gently,

"Do you think that God would want you to continue in work for Him that didn't feel right for you? He would want you to fulfil your life here on earth by doing work that filled you with joy. A priest who no longer wanted to be a priest would not be effective and his unhappiness would become noticeable to his parishioners."

"But how can I go back on promises?"

"You can explain to God that now you have found your true vocation you would like to give yourself to that."

"But chastity, poverty and obedience would not be part of my life as a lay person and they are the very things that I've promised."

"You made the promises when you became a priest as part of your priesthood. If you are no longer a priest then the vows are no longer relevant."

Patrick was shocked. He hadn't seen it from that point of view. The fear and tension that had surrounded his decision dropped away. He'd been a square peg in a round hole for so long that he now embraced the thorough roundness of the new slot that he so comfortably fitted into at the sound of those words.

He had no money and nowhere to live. What he needed, he decided, was some kind of accreditation which would enable him to be taken seriously in the area that he hoped to work in and with that in mind he applied for an appropriate training course. They couldn't teach him anything that he didn't already know, of course but he just needed the Certificate, the bit of paper that would provide the credibility for his new ambitions. The College he chose was at Westerbridge, he was accepted and he would start there in September. He would pick up casual work in the meantime to make ends meet. The excitement and freedom he felt were similar to the feelings he'd had when his Youth Club became so successful. He wasn't sure how he'd have coped if his parents had still been alive. Their, at least his mother's, huge disappointment would have cowed him and possibly even deterred him but here he was now, free, free to do whatever he wanted and in whatever way he wanted to do it.

*

The school spring term was short as Easter was late and soon it was the summer holidays again, a whole year since the lido and polio. Released from their summer exams and having had yet another birthday, David and Judy swung through the warm days with a feeling of utter liberation. David was relieved that the term had been short because the return to a full-time busy, noisy school had exhausted him. They strolled along their old walk-ways by the brook from Alma Park to the river. It was like old times yet not like old times. They decided to roll down the hill just like they had done when they were children, lying with their hands straight above their heads and their legs straight. They rolled away colliding and parting, colliding again and laughing at their return to childhood. They finally came to rest inches apart and facing each other. They lay there in the warmth, chuckling until David stroked her hair again and instead of the little kisses he'd given her on her forehead and cheeks before, he reached for her lips. It was a short kiss, you could even say a chaste kiss, but the difference between a forehead or a cheek and lips was electrifyingly noticeable to both of them. They jumped up and continued walking by the river quietly as if nothing had happened. But everything had happened. They eventually glanced at each other and stopped where the river widened and the trees clustered at the edge of the bank. Their lips touched again. Everything around them seemed to suddenly take on a greater clarity. The colours became more brilliant, the daisies whiter, the fields greener, the trees, more strongly outlined against the blue sky and the hum of the bees, a song. Nothing would ever be the same again.

*

One Saturday, Patrick Conti approached Joe's house hoping that he'd be in. He hadn't been in touch and had decided to just turn up. He rang the door bell and waited. Sandra answered the door and stood for a moment, not recognising the tall, gaunt man with the weathered face who stood before her.

"Sandra! Hello after all this time. Sorry I couldn't let you know I was coming. I hope it isn't inconvenient."

Sandra felt sick when she realised it was Patrick. What was he doing here?

"Patrick?"

"Have I changed so much that you didn't recognise your old Patrick?"

Sandra felt herself backing away. He wasn't "her old Patrick" anymore. Joe heard talking on the doorstep and came to see who it was.

"Patrick! My goodness, what a surprise! Don't stand there, come in!"

Joe seemed genuinely pleased to see him so Patrick went in, relieved but not looking forward to what he had to tell them. He didn't like the look on Sandra's face for a start. It was approaching lunchtime and he was pressed to stay. He'd been hoping that he could stay for a while and needed no encouragement to do so. During lunch Sandra sat silently, not joining in with the conversation. Joe was eager to find out what had happened to Patrick during his years away and neither of them noticed Sandra's silence.

After lunch Sandra explained that she had to go out, although there was in fact no need for her to go anywhere and she left Joe and Patrick alone. It was then that Patrick gave his news to Joe. He was leaving the priesthood and hoped to work with young people. In one way Joe was shocked as he'd thought of his brother as a priest for years now but in another way, Joe wasn't surprised because he'd always had doubts about Patrick's vocation. Nevertheless, it was big news for Joe to take in and he felt strange as he considered it, especially as it looked as if this brother whom he hadn't seen for years would now be living not far away.

"So where's this nephew of mine? I was glad to hear from your letter that he was recovering. How is he?"

"Yes, thank God, he's better. He's out with a friend at the moment."

"So will I be handing over the Conti chalice to him?" Patrick said, with something of a smirk.

Joe was finding it difficult to talk to Patrick. He seemed to be a bit too flippant considering the enormity of what he'd done. Joe had always been a bit wary of Patrick but couldn't quite put his finger on it. He remembered that when they were young, Patrick was good company, energetic and humorous but self-satisfied and too pleased by his own popularity. He had an ineffable quality of attraction as if he could cast a spell and draw people to him. When he'd become a priest Joe had presumed that Patrick would grow out of his arrogance through the seriousness of his studies and position and perhaps a little humility might take its place but on the one occasion when he'd visited them he found that Patrick to be still his old self. He was due to start his course soon so perhaps they wouldn't see much of him. Nevertheless, Joe invited him to stay on for dinner and so Patrick was still sitting comfortably when Sandra returned. Joe could see that Sandra, too, was finding Patrick's presence difficult. Was it just because they hadn't seen him for so long or was it because his presence filled the room?

David came home to find his mythical Uncle Patrick alive and well and sitting in his living room. He had never met him and was intrigued to see a slightly older version of his own father. Patrick showed a great interest in David. They exchanged information on the illnesses and rehabilitation that they'd both undergone during the same time period but unknown to each other and Patrick regaled David with stories from the missions and his life in Africa. He didn't mention his time as a parish priest or his exile to the monastery. He spoke of the course that he would be doing in Westerbridge but both Sandra and David presumed that the Church was sending him there as part of his work as a priest. Joe wondered how they would react when they knew the truth and wished that Patrick would tell them himself. He watched as David was lured into Patrick's web of charm. Despite his physical and mental torment over the past two years, Patrick hadn't as yet, lost his strong, magnetic personality. Joe was taken back to their younger days when he, the quiet one, was hidden in the shadow of this big brother. He didn't want to go back to those days and he didn't want David to become ensnared and perhaps lured into the same mistake that Patrick had made.

As Sandra hadn't yet heard Patrick's news she told him that David had been blessed with a vocation just as he himself had. She was surprised by the silence that this comment produced from all three of them. She'd imagined that Patrick would be delighted by the continuance of the family tradition and would be a good guide for David, taking him under his wing. She'd imagined that David would be happy to have a mentor so close to home. She sat bewildered. Joe felt that this was the opportune moment for Patrick to explain that he considered himself to be no longer a priest but to Joe's annoyance he just looked at David and said how happy he would be to hand over the precious chalice. It appeared that Patrick was leaving it to Joe to break the news, escaping the horror that his decision would cause or as he would probably call it, their lack of understanding.

When Patrick had gone, Joe lost no time in telling them that Patrick had decided to leave the priesthood. He didn't want any more embarrassing comments about priests and blessings. Sandra and David were stunned. Sandra was particularly disturbed, in fact, angry. She had been very much in love with Patrick and deeply hurt by his deceitful omission in telling her of his plans to become a priest. She re-lived the scene of his mother warning her off; the shock at hearing that he was going to be a priest. That's when she'd turned her attention to Joe whom she now admitted to herself she hadn't loved a fraction as much as she'd loved Patrick. And now here was Patrick coming into their house and announcing that he was no longer a priest. It was all too late. The loss and waste of her life crippled her. She could tell none of this to Joe of course. The love she'd felt for Patrick turned to fury and hatred would soon take its place. She blamed him for her boring life with Joe, for the loss of vibrancy in her life, for the dead future that lay ahead when she could have had a lively, exciting life with Patrick if only he'd realised that he hadn't wanted to be a priest all those years ago. But all she said in response to the news was,

"Do you know why he's given up his vocation?"

"He didn't explain."

"And you didn't ask him? Surely that would be the first thing you'd say after being given that kind of news."

She was annoyed that she didn't know the reason for Patrick's decision. Perhaps when he was younger he had truly believed that he had a vocation. But then, she asked herself, why did he behave in the way he did? The way he had behaved with her was not the way that a man intending to be a priest would behave. She was so confused and angry that she didn't dare say anymore.

David was shocked too. He was also in the throes of battling with what he'd thought was a vocation. The thrill of meeting his uncle had turned into something else. He wanted answers.

Chapter 15

The surge in demand for university places had left the University of Westerbridge with a dilemma. The small, compact cathedral city of Westerbridge allowed no room for expansion. The University was in search of further premises when news of the sale of "The Oaks" became known. The mansion and grounds were snapped up and refurbishment began immediately. Rita and Edward, Jane and Freddie who had hoped to create studios for artists there cancelled their public meeting and their "Save The Oaks" campaign. Although they were at least relieved that "The Oaks" would not be torn down, they were disappointed that their plans and hopes would not materialise. During the year, as the university planned and designated the various spaces to the Faculties in need of expansion, Rita heard through her extensive grapevine that it had became clear that for the time being the Coach House, Stables and Orangery would not be needed and as they were separate from the main building they were to be rented to organisations or companies until the university had need of them.

The little group applied for the lease on the Coach House and the Stables and work began on their plans for the studios, having obtained grants from an Art Society and a Historic House Preservation

Trust. Jane Stevens was the first person to rent a studio and space was rented by Freddie for exhibitions. Rita made sure that "County Life" made a feature of the "The Oaks Studios" in its next edition and in less than a year the studios took off and became well-known locally.

*

Jane invited Judy to go along with her and Richard when she set up her new studio. Judy replied that she'd love to but she'd arranged to meet David which led to David being invited too. It felt very strange to be going back to "The Oaks". Each one of them had a connection with the place. It was a particularly poignant moment for David when they drove down the drive and the splendid house came into view. He re-lived arriving there in an ambulance, followed by months of therapy and separation from all that he was used to. But what he mainly remembered and felt again were the electric times with Judy on the bank of the river with the dragonflies, the geese, the soft, warm breezes when he'd realised that he could never part from her and the disentanglement of his opposing desires had begun.

It was a poignant moment for Judy too as she also re-lived the time spent apart from her soul-mate and the spell that the river bank and the meadows had cast over them.

For Richard, it brought back the memory of his self-inflicted loneliness and hibernation from the world before the astonishing reunion with Edward which in turn led him to meeting Jane. Jane was the only one of the group who had no prior memories of "The Oaks" but had the place to thank for her meeting with Richard through Edward.

Judy helped Jane arrange her materials while David and Richard strolled in the gardens, each dwelling on the time when they had lived there.

Richard was aware of David's reverie as they walked along the bank towards the fields where last year Rita and Edward had found a space for each other. He decided not to interrupt David's thoughts and entered into his own reverie. He was on the verge of asking Jane to marry him. They were very different people and Richard wondered whether if they married, those differences could eventually cause problems. He was quite a bit older than Jane too so would that be a problem? He realised that the answers to those questions would only unfold if they were actually married and would certainly never be solved by ruminating on them in isolation. His mind was made up.

The Orangery was now a café and the four had lunch together looking over the gardens.

"I'm trying to persuade David to try for Oxford when the time comes." Richard told them, glancing at David and smiling.

"Surely you wouldn't need persuading." Jane said. "All those dreaming spires. What more could you ask for?"

David knew what more he could ask for but didn't say.

"What's stopping you?" Jane went on relentlessly, as she always did when another person would have stopped. She never acted as an angel fearing to tread.

David couldn't respond but as they were all staring at him waiting for a reply he just said,

"It's complicated."

When they got back home, Tim invited Jane and Richard to go in for a drink and Judy and David disappeared. There was an outhouse at the back of 2, Sebastopol Terrace which had once been the outside toilet and wash house. Judy had made it into her studio with a trestle table for all her art materials. It was too cold in the winter but was adequate for the rest of the time. Having just left Jane's real studio she commented that she now felt a bit stupid that she was calling this old wash house a studio. David remarked that Jane's studio used to be a stable so what was the difference?

They flopped down on the cushions and David grabbed her arm.

"I've got some massive news. Uncle Patrick turned up at our house and when he'd gone Dad told us that he'd stopped being a priest! I can't believe it. How can you stop being a priest?"

"What on earth made him do that? Did he say why? Is he still ill?"

"Dad said he didn't explain."

"That's amazing, really odd. Are you going to try and find out why?"

"I don't think I could, I hardly know him."

"I'd love to know what would make a priest give it all up."

They went on to discuss whether David should follow Richard's advice, work hard and try for Oxford. David said that he wasn't sure because of the complications.

"What are these complications?" Judy asked.

"If you still want to go to Art College, we'll have to find out if there's one there in Oxford so we can still be together. Could you ask Miss Stevens?"

"I'll do that next time I see her."

The next time they saw her was only a few minutes later when Tim was leading them into the garden to have their drinks in the sunshine.

"Judy, I didn't know you had a studio too!" Jane exclaimed.

Judy looked embarrassed but David asked if there was an Art College in Oxford. Jane and Richard understood immediately the implication of this question and Jane replied that yes, there was one and she had no doubt that Judy would get in when the time came. David glanced at Richard and they both smiled, knowing that David would now accept the extra tutoring that Richard had offered him.

When the three adults had settled themselves in the garden Jane commented that David and Judy were exceptionally close for two such young people and was shocked to hear that they had been inseparable since the age of five.

"It's most unusual", she continued. "I wonder what the connection is that has kept them so close over all those years."

"I really don't know." Tim replied. "Our two families didn't even know each other. In fact it was a good few years before I met Sandra and Joe. I've always felt that Sandra wasn't keen on them being friends but I might be wrong."

"Perhaps she just wanted him to have a broader group of friends." Jane suggested

"Well, he was on the football team, still is, now that his leg's improved so much. So he had a big group of friends from there. But he always spent his spare time with Judy. It was always just at school that other friends came into the picture."

Jane forged ahead "What about his vocation to be a priest that Sandra is always bringing up?"

"As far as I know, that's still there. He said that he's always wanted to be a priest for as long as he can remember."

"I suppose there's a lot of family influence going on there." Jane mused.

Richard decided to change the subject. He'd grown close to David at "The Oaks" and was aware that David had done a lot of thinking while he was convalescing. He felt that his discussions with David were as sacrosanct as the confessional and he wouldn't enter into any gossip about him. But from the garden, the group couldn't see into the wash house where childish companionship was turning into adolescent desire.

*

The following Monday David was called into the Headmaster's study. The priest was sitting behind his desk, slowly taking off his glasses as David was shown in.

"It has come to my attention that you are walking with a girl and holding her hand on your way to school. Is this correct?"

"Yes, Father."

"Why are you doing this?"

"We've been doing it since we were five years old, Father. It's just natural for us."

The Head seemed to soften a little.

"Ah, I see. She's a relative? You are responsible for making sure she gets to school safely?"

"No, Father, she's not a relative."

"So, I repeat my question – why are you and she holding hands?"

David's imaginary answer was that it was none of his business and he could do what he wanted when not at school. He could feel anger rising in him but knew that he must not express it. He was afraid of this person who had the power to expel him. He stood meekly before the Headmaster.

"We're very old friends and have always held hands."

"Well it stops now. Do you understand?"

No, David didn't understand. How dare this person interfere with his life?

The Headmaster seemed to have read his thoughts.

"When you are in school uniform you are representing this school and fourteen- year old pupils do not march around the town hanging onto a girl."

David said nothing, hoping that his anger was not showing on his face.

"Do you know what a "dangerous occasion of sin is?"

"Yes, Father."

"Tell me what you think it is."

David parroted the catechism answer.

"I'm pleased that you know the catechism but would you explain it in your own words so that I know that you have understood?"

"It's when a place or a person might lead you into sin and so you must avoid them."

"Give me an example of a place that might be a dangerous occasion of sin."

"If a man spends all his money on drink and can't feed his children then a pub would be a dangerous of sin."

"Very good. And a person who might be a dangerous occasion of sin?"

David knew what the Head was getting at and refused to play his game.

"If your friend steals from shops and he wants you to do the same you should avoid that person and not be their friend."

The Head had to admit that the example was correct.

"I would like you to tell your father about our conversation and ask him how holding a girl's hand could be a dangerous occasion of sin. Go back to your class."

David left the room, fuming. How could this old man, a priest, know anything about holding a girl's hand?

At Saint Catherine's an identical conversation was taking place between Judy and the Reverend Mother, creating similar feelings and responses. They stood at their usual meeting place after school.

"I've been told not to hold your hand." David said.

"Me, too." Judy replied.

"Really? That means that whoever reported us knows who we both are. Let's go to the barn and decide what to do. But just for now we'd better not hold hands because they'll be watching us."

In the barn, they sat on the old beam that had fallen in. David took hold of Judy's hand. She placed her other hand on top of his and said,

"We've always held hands. It's nothing new. It's so natural that we just do it without even thinking. Why should we change that just because two old people who've never done it don't like it?"

David smiled and leaned over.

"Because it's a dangerous occasion of sin and could lead to this."

And kissed her.

It had always been natural for them to be easy with each other; bodies colliding as they rolled down hills, a kiss on a cut or a graze, a hug for a triumph, a casual arm over a shoulder. They wouldn't stop now even though they were both aware that these marks of affection had taken on a different colour. They both agreed that holding hands and kissing were not sins.

*

Jane, Freddie Alexander, Rita and Edward had formed a small charity to run the Studios and had decided that as none of them had the time themselves to run the Studios they would need a part-time administrator/manager, preferably a volunteer. No-one came forward to do the work freely so they reluctantly advertised the post, hoping that their grants would stretch to it.

Patrick Conti, no longer Father Conti, had thrilled at the thought of freedom when he'd finally decided to leave the priesthood. But where was that freedom now? he asked himself. He was just adrift in a world that he didn't recognise anymore. He missed the community and camaraderie of his fellow priests, the well-defined structure of his life and most of all he missed the feeling that his calling had been truly from God which had given him his energy and enthusiasm. He walked through his days with the very same glazed, empty expression that he had seen in his parishioners and which had set off his disbelief in the efficacy of what he was doing. It also hit him as a surprise that he hadn't already realised that his desire to work with young people had been to draw them into the Church. If he took up that work again what would be his motive this time? How could he draw them into the church if he was no longer a priest? And why would he? He'd been convinced that his priestly powers would remain within him but that had turned out not to be so. He was dead inside. He was well into his course at Westerbridge University by now so he thought that he might as well finish it and gain his bit of paper. He was living on a University grant and was fortunate to have been allocated one of the few rooms available to mature students in the Hall of Residence. However, he needed more money, especially as he ran a car and didn't want to give up this slice of freedom. He was sitting in the refectory having a break when he noticed a local paper that had been left on the table. It was there that he found Rita's advert for the part-time work managing the Studios. He would have time for that as he was free at the weekends and in the evenings. He acknowledged to himself that he had free time because he had no friends and nowhere to go. He hadn't gone back to Joe's because he could see that Joe had his own life and Sandra didn't seem to want him there. He lost no time in applying for the job and posted it to the Regent Square address.

A few days after the deadline for the applications the Trustees, Jane, Freddie, Rita and Edward met to consider the applications. Rita looked at them, bemused.

"We only have one application, possibly because it's part-time, not much pay and out in the wilds. But what's more peculiar is who the person is who's applied – Patrick Conti. Freddie, I think you've met Patrick's brother, Joe and the rest of us all know Joe. But Patrick's a priest and the last we'd heard of him was that he'd been in Africa and was very ill."

They all looked bemused too, especially Jane who had clear memories of the good-looking priest of her Youth Club days.

"Have any of you heard anything about him recently?" Rita added. "It's strange because you know that I work quite closely with Sandra and she didn't mention not only that he's better but that he's in the area."

Joe hadn't mentioned his brother's return to Edward either, when they met to play chess; particularly not that he'd left the priesthood. He wanted to let the news settle down in himself before he could talk about it to anyone else. David had told Judy about his Uncle Patrick's visit but she'd forgotten to mention it to Tim or Rita, having other things on her mind. He hadn't come again and the memory had faded.

"What shall we do?" said Rita. "We only have this one application but it seems a bit odd that a priest has applied. Surely he has enough work to do already."

Freddie made a suggestion.

"I'm the only one here who doesn't know the family well so shall I interview him? If he's suitable do you trust my judgement to give him the job or turn him down?"

They agreed and a letter was sent to Patrick asking him to meet Freddie at the Viridian Gallery.

Patrick went along for his interview with some resentment. It was a long time since anyone had looked him over to decide whether he was worthy. In his present state of mind he knew that he would come over badly in an interview. He managed to dredge up the feeling that he used to have of himself as being a sociable, energetic, strong, capable but most of all, popular person. He strode along trying to fit himself back into his old self-image. Freddie was intrigued by what he'd heard of Patrick and was looking forward to meeting him. There was no mistaking him when he walked into the gallery, the family resemblance to Joe and David being unmistakable.

Freddie had wondered whether to tell Patrick that he had met his brother on several occasions but decided to play it by ear. When he was asked why he wanted the job Patrick just told the truth. He was on a course and although he had a grant he needed a bit of extra money, especially as he wanted to keep his car. His CV had included social work both here and in Africa and his work running a Youth Club but had not declared that this work had been done as a priest. Freddie presumed to himself that by social work Patrick meant parish work. He hadn't actually lied. Freddie drove him to the Studios to explain what would be required and decided that if Patrick still wanted the job he would give it to him. Freddie's easy charm and his deferential manner towards him had enabled Patrick to summon up the person he used to be and his manner became more expansive as they chatted on their way to "The Oaks". Patrick was offered the job and he accepted.

Jane Stevens, still only part-time at St. Catherine's, was working in her studio when they arrived and not by accident. She was introduced to Patrick but to his horror or amazement she said that they'd already met. He knew he would not have forgotten such a beautiful woman if he had ever met her and he protested that she must have mistaken him for someone else.

"It was a long time ago, so you won't remember me. I was just a teenager. I went to your Youth Club, your very successful Youth Club. It was never the same after you left."

It was horror not amazement. He was keeping it quiet that he'd been a priest although he wasn't quite sure why. Was it because you are usually a priest for life? You can't really say that you *were* a priest, it doesn't make sense. Was it because he didn't want people to think that he was a disgraced priest, perhaps that he'd been de-frocked? He should come clean. He'd thought that eventually his past would catch up with him but certainly not this quickly. His parish had not been in this area. This was a fluke. It knocked him off balance but he noticed that Jane hadn't mentioned that he'd been a priest, didn't comment on his lack of the long, black cassock and dog collar that he'd worn when she last knew him. This really was too much to take in and he was pleased when Freddie said that it was time to go back.

Patrick started to get to grips with what was required of him at the Studios on the following Saturday. Jane was there again but this time she was with a man and Patrick's own nephew and a girl. David greeted him in surprise and then introduced him to Judy and Richard Jackson but he was baffled when he heard that Patrick was doing some work for them. Judy and David went to wander by the river.

"So that's Uncle Patrick. He does look just like you and your Dad. Very handsome."

David grinned. "It's out Italian ancestry."

You haven't talked much about being a priest yourself lately." Judy said with a searching look.

"I know. It's all mixed up now."

"What do you mean?"

"I'm not sure anymore that I want to be a priest."

Judy stared at him.

"The other day at school we were reading a passage from "Hebrews" and it said "Never will I leave you; never will I forsake you" and it felt as if I was saying it to you. If being a priest means that I can't be with you anymore then I'm not going to be a priest."

This time, his doubt didn't open up a pit of fire; the Gates of Hell didn't start to open because they both knew that it was the truth.

*

Patrick worked out that Jane Stevens was at the Studios every Thursday and he made sure that he "accidently" coincided with her time there. They quite often had a break together in the café and she would chat with her usual openness and humour. On one occasion when he popped his head round her door and said that he was ready for a break she decided that this would be her opportunity to find out why a priest was doing this work or possibly find out that he was no longer a priest. She said she was ready for a break too and they walked over to the café.

"Patrick, when I knew you a long time ago, you were a priest. Am I right in thinking that you're no longer a priest or are you on some sort of sabbatical? She asked in her forthright manner.

"I'm no longer a priest, Jane. Well some people think that once you're a priest, you are always a priest. It's not something that you can retire from so shall I just say that I am not acting as a priest anymore."

In her usual way, treading where angels would fear to go, Jane asked the awful question.

"Why?"

"It's too complicated."

"Sorry, I shouldn't have asked."

"It's ok."

Patrick held her gaze for a moment too long and she said she must get back to her work. There was an exhibition coming up and she had a lot to do. Patrick ignored her desire to go and asked her who Richard Jackson was who had been in the Studio the first time he'd visited after taking on the job.

"Richard's my boyfriend. I suppose at our age "boyfriend" sounds silly but I don't think there's another word."

"Beau? Lover? Sweetheart?"

Jane felt uncomfortable and repeated her need to finish her work.

The following Thursday, he was back at "The Oaks" as usual and came into Jane's Studio on the pretext of seeing her work for the exhibition. His emptiness disappeared when he was with her. They stood together looking at her latest painting but Patrick was looking at her not the painting. He put his hand on her cheek, tracing her cheekbone. He then wrapped a curl round his finger and whispered,

"You're a very special person, Jane."

He'd left the room before she could react. She stood by the table, still feeling his touch on her cheek, wondering how she would have responded if he hadn't left so abruptly. She was aware that she was still attracted to him, just as she had been when she was teenager and she'd been in awe of this unusual priest. As a priest he'd been unattainable but now, now what? But there was something disturbing about Patrick, a darkness, well hidden but that Jane had picked up.

Richard had come to the Studio to pick Jane up just as Patrick left but not before Richard had seen the affectionate scene as he passed the window. His heart sank. He had decided a while ago to ask Jane to marry him but had still not found the perfect moment and now it looked as if his procrastination could have cost him this lovely woman.

"I've just seen Patrick Conti leaving. It's strange that you two have met again after all that time. I remember your surprise when his name came up once when we were at Rita's."

"Yes, it was really strange to hear that name again and find out that Joe's his brother. What a small world!"

"Do you know what his plans are? Is he going to stay in this area after he's finished at the university?"

"I don't know." Jane answered as she picked up her bag and walked to the door.

Richard followed, not knowing how to continue the conversation. He felt his life slipping back into the lonely space he'd so recently vacated. He recalled how his first love had been stolen by a GI and now Jane was about to be stolen too from right under his nose. He wondered what to do. Do you propose and snatch the girl back, risking that she might already prefer the other man or do you wait and see what happens? It was too late now to do what he should have done. As soon as he knew that he wanted to marry her, then he should have asked her. It was his own fault.

"You're very quiet." Jane said as they drove back.

"I'm just thinking."

"You're always thinking."

"I know and that's the problem. Thinking and not acting."

"What do you mean?"

He continued driving, deciding that his slowness and dithering were going to cost him dearly.

"Quite a while ago, I decided that I wanted to marry you and that I was going to propose but I was waiting for the perfect moment. I was also worried that if you said no then I supposed that would be the end of our relationship and I couldn't bear the thought of not being with you anymore."

He risked a glance at her and was surprised to see that she was smiling.

"Richard, I've been waiting for ages for you to propose and I'm still waiting."

He stopped the car.

"But I thought, I thought …"

"What did you think?"

"I thought you were seeing quite a bit of Patrick Conti, getting close…."

"Richard, listen. Patrick is attractive, yes, and he's good company, but there's something a bit flaky about him, something unsettling, something almost unstable. I'm not interested in him in that way."

"So would you...."

"I'm still waiting." She laughed.

*

All the Studios had been taken and Rita decided that it was time to bring everyone together to meet and socialise. She planned one of her Wine Evenings where she would invite old and new acquaintances and friends to mingle for potential mutual benefit. Judy and David arrived first, having just been to the cinema to celebrate their fifteenth birthdays. Rita thought how it didn't seem long since they had come separately, David attached to Sandra's apron strings and Judy running around in whatever clothes Tim had had time to wash. They were now what seemed to be typical 1960s teenagers much to Sandra's distaste. Sandra felt that the world was turning upside down. David hadn't spoken about being a priest for a long time and Joe had forbidden her to bring it up. When asked by anyone what he wanted to do after school he would reply that he was hoping to go to Oxford.

When Sandra saw Patrick come in and be greeted by Rita she was knocked off balance. No news of his job at the Studios had reached her and she wondered why he was there and how he knew Rita. She also wondered how it was that Rita knew her brother-in-law and hadn't mentioned it. She watched as Patrick walked boldly up to Jane Stevens. He seemed to know her too. She noticed how closely he was standing next to Jane, how he touched her arm as he spoke. But she also noticed Jane backing away and looking relieved when Richard came back into the room. Sandra was both fascinated and resentful. Obviously there was a lot going on that she didn't know about. It was bad enough that David was still spending all his time with the voodoo princess.

"You're deep in thought." Said Joe when he came back with the drinks.

"I don't understand what Patrick's doing here. How does he know Rita?"

"Edward's just told me that Patrick's managing the new Studios. It's just part-time." Without being seen, David and Judy helped themselves to some wine and made their way to the summer house in the copse. They sipped the wine and giggled, neither of them being used to alcohol. Guests were spilling out of Rita's to have a cigarette or have some fresh, summer air.

"Let's go to the barn. There are too many people around." David suggested.

It was still light as they made their way along the brook to the river, sipping their illicit drinks. They reached their barn where they flopped down on straw and blankets that they'd taken there once to make it more comfortable. They started to talk about the future but gradually the barrier that they'd both tacitly placed on going further than kisses broke away. They lay together, as the Bible might have put it, while a red sunset streaked across the sky as the geese came home for the night. The river flowed on by, undisturbed in its pursuit of the sea. The moon pulled at the earth and the oceans responded.

Sandra hadn't noticed David and Judy slipping out because she was watching Patrick with the eye of a hawk. As soon as she saw him go outside she quickly followed

"So you're not a priest anymore. How does that work?"

Patrick, lighting a cigarette looked up to see Sandra standing over him.

"Oh, so Joe's told you."

"It's a pity it took you so long to realise that you shouldn't have been a priest."

Patrick was shocked by the harshness of her tone.

"What do you mean?"

"What do I mean? Have you forgotten? We only split up because your mother wanted you to be a priest."

"Split up?"

"Do I have to spell it out? We were boyfriend and girlfriend when your mother announced that you were going to be a priest, something that had obviously slipped your mind when we were together. But that's a small thing compared to what you did afterwards when you were actually a priest."

He was aware that she'd been drinking and wondered where all this was leading.

"You were on leave; you had nowhere to go so you came and stayed with us for a few days. Ring any bells?"

Her voice was getting louder.

"Sandra. What can I say? I didn't force you; you were willing, more than willing, in fact."

"But you were a priest. You broke your vows. We didn't get chance to talk about it afterwards and I want an answer. Was it because you still loved me?"

Patrick couldn't remember ever having loved her.

"But Sandra, it was years ago. Why are you bringing this up now?"

"Because I've always wondered."

"A priest is still a man. A man has needs, that's all. It's as simple as that."

"So that's all it was? I just fulfilled your need? I just happened to be there?" She spat out.

It was a relief for her in a way. The spell that Patrick's memory had had over her was broken. She'd lived for years wondering what her life would have been like if things had been different, years comparing her life now with the imaginary life that she'd conjured up for herself when she'd thought that she and Patrick had a future together. He was the man she'd broken her marriage vows for and she was the woman that he'd broken his priestly vows for. Did that mean nothing to him? Obviously not. For the first time she saw him clearly – selfish, shallow, arrogant.

"Did you tell Joe?" Patrick asked, worried about the consequences of that although Joe had welcomed him when he went to visit them so perhaps she hadn't.

All he cares about is himself, she thought. Well, he can stew in hell.

Joe had been having a long chat with Edward when he saw Sandra come in through the french windows. She didn't look well and she asked him if they could go home. She was close to tears as she looked at the man who'd stayed by her while she carped and complained about everything because she'd been secretly comparing him to the imaginary picture she'd had of his brother. She looked at Joe with a new understanding.

Judy and David had fallen asleep. Owls screeching around the barn woke them. It was pitch black as they fumbled around for their clothes. David found her hand and squeezed. She looked small and defenceless as she lay on the straw and he scooped her up and held her close.

"Don't forget – never will I leave you; never will I forsake you."

They decided to go straight home, not back to the party. David waited while she let herself into number 2 and then walked briskly back home. He was surprised to see that his parents were already home as Rita's parties were famous for going on into the early hours. Joe realised that when they left the party he hadn't looked for David to tell him they were going. Sandra had seemed so exhausted and strange that he'd just wanted to get her home.

"Sorry we left without telling you. Your Mum's not well so we came home."

David was glad that Joe hadn't thought to tell him because he would have discovered that he wasn't there.

"It's ok. It was too hot and noisy so we left too."

David went to bed and thought over all that happened that night. Nothing would ever be the same again.

The party was still flowing. Patrick was continuing his pursuit of Jane Stevens. He knew that he would make a better partner for her than Richard and all he had to do was to prove it to her. When

Richard was in deep conversation with Edward he moved over to Jane. Whenever he was feeling comfortable, his despondency and emptiness disappeared, giving place to his favourite persona – the popular, sociable man who could draw people to him by sheer force of his personality. He didn't remember Jane from the Youth Club. She would have been one of the many girls who'd gathered round him. He basked in his former glory as he asked Jane about her exhibition which had just opened that morning. He said he was looking forward to seeing it when he was next at the Studios. He was looking down on her as he spoke and his eyes stayed on hers for too long as they had done at the Studio. She felt the same discomfort, almost fear. She called Freddie over,

"Patrick's asking how the exhibition's going."

She excused herself and left the two talking, much to Patrick's annoyance.

Chapter 16

Tim picked up the letter from the doormat. He recognised the postmark but not the handwriting. It was from the town where Marie lived in her enclosed convent. He didn't want Judy to see it or it might start the argument again about her wanting to meet her mother. She hadn't mentioned it for a long time and he was hoping that she'd let it drop. It wasn't until he was at work that he opened the letter to find that it was from Marie's Mother Superior informing him that Marie was seriously ill. He could visit her if he so wished and she gave the address of the hospital. There was no indication of what the illness was, whether Marie was dying, whether he should go as soon as possible. It was a formal, frustrating letter.

After work he called in at Rita's. He told her about the letter and that he needed to go and visit Marie but without Judy knowing where he was going. Rita replied that they going over to the Studios on Saturday and she was thinking of inviting Judy to go with them so he should plan to go then. The plan went ahead and Tim found himself confronting a grim Victorian hospital just half a mile's walk from the centre of the town. He was led into a side room where he found Marie's light frame propped up in bed. He was surprised to see that she looked exactly as he remembered her even though it was well over a decade since he'd seen her. He worked out that she must be in her early thirties but she looked like a child. Perhaps living without stress, talking to God all day and having everything provided for you was what kept you young he thought as he took the chair next to the bed.

"Thank you for coming, Tim. I know I don't deserve it. Please tell me how Judy is?"

There were tears in her eyes as she listened to Judy's accomplishments.

"She's done very well in her exams and she'll be going into sixth form in September. She's very good at art and hoping to go to Art College. Oh, and she's got a boyfriend. He's a very old friend, right from childhood but that's grown into a romance."

He smiled, not sure whether Marie would approve. But she'd asked about Judy so he ploughed on.

"Yes, David, David Conti, a very nice young man and I …."

Marie was so startled that the drip was nearly ripped from her arm as she tried to raise herself.

"Did you say Conti?"

"Yes, it's an unusual name, isn't it? Italian."

"Does he have a relative called Patrick who's a priest?"

"Yes, what a small world! Do you know him? But I should say that he *was* a priest. He no longer practises as a priest is how he describes his resignation."

Marie's agitation was beyond what Tim could understand. She was catching her breath and sobbing.

"Shall I get a nurse?" He asked, standing up, not knowing how to deal with this strange display caused by the name Conti."

"No." She stopped and lay back, silent for what felt like an eternity.

"Now that he's no longer a priest I'm released from my secret and free to tell you. Patrick Conti is Judy's father."

Utter confusion was the first feeling that hit Tim, followed by anger.

They were quiet for a while and then it was as if Marie drew strength and in a cold, dispassionate way told Tim what had happened.

"Do you remember when I used to go to my cousins for the holidays? It was to give you and Agnes some time for yourselves but I enjoyed going. There was a Youth Club in the town that my cousins went to and they took me along. It was run by Father Conti. I was flattered when he took an interest in me because he was very popular and looked like a film star. We used to go to his church too. One late afternoon I was in the church on my own lighting candles for Mum and Dad when he came in. I was crying because I missed Mum and Dad and felt a bit adrift. He took me into the Vestry and was very kind and loving towards me and it just sort of went on from there. I knew that sex before marriage was wrong and I knew that he'd taken a vow of chastity so that's when I decided to spend the rest of my life atoning for enabling a priest to break his vows."

"Enabling a priest to break his vows? For heaven's sake, Marie, he broke them himself. He was a mature man taking advantage of a naïve young girl! He had power and authority over you. He was totally to blame!"

"I didn't see it like that. I had a choice. He didn't force me."

"He didn't need to force you because he knew how to seduce you. He knew you'd be putty in his hands."

"When I found I was pregnant I refused to say who the father was because if that meant he had to leave the priesthood that would have meant that not only had I helped him to break a vow he'd made to God but the Church would have lost a priest."

As Marie fell back onto the pillows Tim sat in silence. He couldn't think straight.

"So you wasted your life for the sake of a despicable man."

"No. I really did want to be a nun. Do you remember I worked at the library for a while because I was too young to enter a convent?

"Yes, but then you had a boyfriend, someone called Freddie?"

"Yes, Freddie Alexander."

Tim couldn't take anymore. He thought about how long he'd known Freddie through Rita, how they'd dined, laughed, chatted and all along he'd been the boyfriend who she'd never taken home, never even given his surname and who Tim had presumed was Judy's father. As it turned out, it had been a blessing that he hadn't known his name or he might have had a very awkward conversation with him. But Tim still didn't know that Judy had already done that and that she had even told Freddie Marie's story.

Marie closed her eyes and seemed to drift away. A nurse came in and suggested that he should leave as Marie was too weak for long visits. He could come back in the early evening. He tumbled out of the hospital and into the café over the road. He was dazed, unable to take in what he'd heard. Questions poured into his mind. How could he tell Judy the sordid story of how she'd come into being? But even more amazing was the fact that Judy and David had turned out to be cousins. Is that why they'd been so close all these years? Was there a subconscious recognition of the same blood? The most difficult decision was how he was going to deal with this information? He could go on as if nothing had happened; never tell Judy that he now knew who her father was. Or he could tell Joe and ask him what he thought he should do. He could ask Rita and Edward. One thing was for sure – he couldn't shoulder this alone.

He returned to Marie's bedside to find her a little brighter. He wondered whether finally offloading the story had eased her.

"A while ago, Judy asked who her real parents were. She was getting upset about it and I had to tell her the truth. I felt that she had the right to know."

Marie turned her face away.

"Did she blame me for not being there for her, never getting in touch, abandoning her?

"I explained the situation but yes, she was hurt although I think she did understand your position. Could she come and see you?"

It was a while before she answered.

"Perhaps when I'm a bit better. I don't want our first meeting to be in this place."

Marie then explained to Tim that the doctors thought that she might have leukaemia. She said that she felt that she should meet Judy before she died and that was why she had wanted Tim to visit her.

*

Rita arranged a small gathering to celebrate Jane and Richard's engagement. It was just for a few close friends so as Patrick hadn't yet advanced into the inner circle Tim's horror at the thought of coming face to face with him was avoided. During the evening, after the congratulations and the champagne, everyone settled down to talk and as soft music started to play Tim asked Joe if he could speak to him privately about something. Joe was convinced that it was something to do with David and Judy. It was quite clear to everyone now that they were no longer little playmates and he wondered whether Tim was worried about their relationship, as the father of a teenage girl. They sat in the imposing hall where no-one could hear them.

"I don't know how to tell you this, Joe, so I'll just have to come straight out with it. I've just been told by Judy's birth mother that Judy's father is your brother, Patrick."

It takes time to understand what someone has said when what they have said is so utterly nonsensical. Joe knew that he hadn't misheard, he knew that Tim didn't make up stupid stories so how was it that he'd just heard something as outlandish as being told that he was about to take a trip to Mars. His first question reflected his puzzlement over his brother's involvement in this situation.

"Birth mother? I thought Judy didn't know who her mother was?"

"She didn't, but I did."

Tim told Joe the whole story even the added shock of finding out that their friend, Freddie Alexander, had been part of the long, sorry tale. Joe couldn't get to grips with it.

"Patrick's Judy's father? But just a minute, that means that I'm Judy's uncle and good heavens, David's her cousin. Oh Tim, I'm so sorry. I always felt that Patrick sailed into the priesthood without thinking it through. Everyone revered him, even from when he was a child because he spoke of having a vocation. I knew his heart wasn't in it, but I honestly think that he never really thought it through and blindly followed the desires of other people. What shall we do? Do we face Patrick with this; make him face up to his responsibilities? But how would Judy take it? Surely such a story would devastate her."

"Yes, I really believe it would."

At that moment David and Judy hurtled through the front door and into the hall where Tim and Joe were sitting. They stopped in their tracks.

"You two look very serious. What's going on?" Asked David.

"Oh, just having a breather." Said Tim. "Perhaps we should go back in and join the party."

"Where've you two been?" Sandra said as they walked back in.

"Just having a chat."

Joe added quietly that he would tell her later. And so he did. Not only did the news confirm for her that Patrick had never felt for her in the way that she'd presumed he had but it was compounded by the fact that she now found herself to be the aunt of the creature who was taking her own son away from the priesthood. She was utterly drained and took to her bed again. Joe thought that as a practising Catholic, Sandra was devastated by the fact that her own brother-in-law had broken his vows to God, had become a fallen priest. Joe was too good and uncomplicated to ever know what was going on.

Later in the week, after more discussion, Joe and Tim finally decided that they would have to tell David and Judy. They felt that they had the right to know but were in fear of delivering the news with its potential consequences. Judy could be fearless and challenging and Tim was afraid that she would challenge Patrick, even publicly if necessary. In the meantime, Tim started to prepare the ground. He told Judy that Marie was in hospital and that he'd been to visit her. She looked at him, stupefied.

"You've been to visit my mother?"

"I couldn't take you for reasons I've already given you. I'd need her permission to take you."

"But she was out of the convent; no-one could have stopped us."

"Remember that I told you how upset she used to get when we took you to visit her when you were a baby."

"What about how upset *I* get when *I* can't see her? That doesn't count does it? It's all about *her* feelings but she's the one who did something wrong, not me."

She stamped off. She was meeting David and told him that she was still being kept away from her mother.

"We could find out which hospital she's in and just go." He suggested.

"I don't know. There's more to it. I can feel it."

They went next door as Richard was taking them over to "The Oaks" to see Jane's exhibition. Even though Patrick knew that Jane had become engaged he was still in pursuit, convinced that he could win her over. He was there when they arrived and Richard sighed at the sight of him hovering over Jane.

"Uncle Patrick!" David called.

They all greeted each other but Patrick was dismayed to see Richard there. He watched as Richard put a proprietary arm around Jane as they walked round the exhibition. They then went to the Orangery for lunch and felt obliged to ask Patrick to join them.

Patrick looked at David. "So when am I going to hand the family chalice over to you, David?"

"Where is this famous chalice, anyway?" Said David, avoiding the question.

"Oh, in a vault somewhere, awaiting your collection." Smiled Patrick.

There was an uneasy silence until Richard looked at his watch and said that they must be going as Tim had asked if Judy and David could be back by 4:30.

"Although he can be good company and he's clearly intelligent and interesting there's something not quite right about Patrick." Jane whispered to Richard as they walked to the car.

"I feel it too." He replied.

Before they'd left for the exhibition Tim had asked Judy and David to come in when they got back from "The Oaks" because he needed to tell them something. They hated being kept in suspense and Judy asked why he couldn't just tell them there and then.

"Because it'll take too long and you have to be at Richard's in a minute."

On the way in the car, they'd wondered what Tim had to say to them. They went through a few possibilities, one of which was the possibility that he knew how far their relationship had developed and they were going to get a father-of-the-girl lecture. It was too toe curling to imagine. When they went in after Richard had dropped them off they were surprised to see that Joe was there too and presumed that their idea was right. But no, what Tim had to tell them was far worse than anything that they could have imagined themselves.

*

Tim warned them that what he had to say was going to be shocking to them. He then told them the whole story of Marie's experience. Shock was too weak a word. It was not just who her father had turned out to be that appalled Judy but the way in which her existence had come about. She shivered at the thought of the scene in the Vestry, her mother discovering she was pregnant but shielding the perpetrator, taking the blame, doing penance for years locked away. She felt tears coming into her eyes. Then the bizarre truth dawned on them both at the same time.

"When we were kids we called ourselves "blood cousins" because we couldn't be blood brothers, being a boy and a girl. And all the time we really were blood cousins." David told Tim and Joe.

In a way, Judy liked the idea that she had the same blood as David, it made them even closer. Their fathers were brothers. She liked the idea despite who the brother was and what he'd done.

"The next thing is: Do we tell Patrick? We must remember that he was never told that he'd fathered a child. To be fair, we don't know how he'd have reacted if he'd been told. For all we know he might have left the church, married Marie and brought you up, Judy, and nobody would have been any the wiser. But, of course, we don't know."

Judy thought about Patrick knowing he was her father. Did she want this man to suddenly start interfering in her life, possibly even coming between her and Tim, claiming rights as the true father?

"No, I don't want him to know. I don't want him in my life."

Tim and Joe breathed a sigh of relief. They had no idea what it would have been like to face Patrick with this charge, no idea how he would have responded, no idea what the knowledge would have led him to do.

"In that case Judy, we'll all keep quiet about it. Do you agree, Joe? David?"

They all agreed.

The news was just too overwhelming. David and Judy went out on their usual walk, silently digesting this extraordinary turn of events. They went into the old barn, their refuge that no-one else seemed to know about and sat facing each other.

"Cousins can still get married." David said.

"We're already married." Smiled Judy.

Once, during their transition from best friends to sweethearts they'd performed their own wedding ceremony but minus priest, registrar or guests. It's in secret like Romeo and Juliet, they'd said to each other. They'd simply told God that they would love Him and each other forever and ever. They were too young to marry but that was because of man-made laws. God knew that it was right for them to be married now. So with a clear conscience they had considered themselves to be above the law of the land and above the rulings of the old Bishops and had both consecrated and consummated their love.

Chapter 17

Patrick was in a desperate state but had yet to realise it. The persona that he stepped into when he was in the company of others successfully masked how he was truly feeling. He'd numbed all memories, all his past was a blacked out sheet. But he didn't appear to have a future either. He still had no real friends, no interests and no hope. He was close to a break down.

    Father Anthony from the monastery in Scotland had kept in touch with him for a while but Patrick's letters in return were fewer until they'd stopped altogether. The monk was aware of Patrick's frail state, the very state that Patrick himself refused to recognise. He knew that Patrick's course was due to finish soon and he accordingly wrote to him to ask him what his next step would be. He added that should Patrick have time between finishing his course and starting his next project he would be very welcome to visit the monastery for a break as their guest. The thought of the peace and beauty of the monastery, the kindness of the monks and the community of Brothers made Patrick weep as he finally let in his despair.

*

Tim went to see Marie again. She was sitting on the chair next to the bed, looking much better. He sat across from her on the other chair.

"I haven't got leukaemia, after all. It was something else that they've managed to put right. I can't remember the name of it, but it doesn't matter because it's all sorted out now."

She seemed remarkably cheerful so Tim decided to put a question to her.

"Are you going to stay at the convent or could you leave now that you know you don't need to do penance for something that wasn't your fault."

"But Tim, I'm not completely exonerated, I did do it, after all, but I take your point. I'm going to do something more useful than I was doing before. I'm going to transfer to an order of nuns who go out into the community and help those in need."

"So you're going to stay being a nun?"

"Yes, my being a nun wasn't part of my penance; I'd always wanted to do that. My atonement was the way in which I did it."

"And Judy? What about your child? Where does she come into it? You've just admitted that you were partly to blame for her existence so what are you going to do about that?"

Tim was starting to feel angry at what he saw as a contradiction. She was going to help people in the community while ignoring her own child.

"Tim, you adopted Judy. You are her father, legally and Agnes was her mother. I was out of the picture. Legally I have no claim on her."

"I'm not talking about legalities. I'm talking about a child's right to know their parents. Judy desperately wants to know you."

"I'm afraid, Tim. That's the truth of it. I'm afraid that my own child will hate me for not being a mother to her."

"We've been through this before. Judy understands the circumstances you were in. She knows you had no option. She just wants to meet you, perhaps keep in touch with you. We can say she's your niece if the convent asks."

"I suppose that's not an outright lie seeing as you and Agnes were her legal parents, by adoption, anyway."

"So what do you say?"

"When I've moved to my new convent I'll send you the address and we'll start from there."

"So it's not a definite no?"

"It's a yes."

He left the hospital with a heart lighter than it been for quite some time.

*

Joe was sitting alone in the living room when Patrick appeared in front of him as if conjured up by the very strength of Joe's thoughts.

"Sorry, did I give you a shock? David let me in on his way out."

It was the first time he'd seen Patrick since Tim had told him Marie's story and he was the last person in the whole world that he would like to have seen at that moment. He was so tempted to tell him that he knew all about his squalid history, how the golden boy had turned so dirty and tarnished but he resisted the satisfaction that would have given him. He had no desire to allow Patrick into Judy and Tim's life and that is exactly what would happen if he faced Patrick with what he'd done.

"You were deep in thought." Said Patrick. "Penny for them."

"You wouldn't want to know." He replied. He closed his eyes. He was so close to telling him.

"Oh, as bad as that, eh? Trouble at work? Arguments with the lovely Sandra? David being naughty?" He asked in his flippant way. He seemed to be in good spirits.

Joe didn't reply. What right did Patrick have to be in good spirits – ever?

"I've just come to tell you something." Patrick continued. "I'm going to Scotland for a break. Not sure when I'll be back."

Joe was relieved to hear that and managed to wish him a good time but didn't offer him tea or coffee or enter into a conversation as to why he was going to Scotland or what he'd be doing there. Patrick felt the coldness and left with a cheerful farewell. He didn't know what was wrong with Joe. Something was eating him, that was for sure. The thought of going to the monastery had cheered Patrick for a while but as he walked through the empty streets back to his lonely room his desolation overcame him again. What right did Joe have for being in such poor spirits? He asked himself. He's got a job, a wife, a son, plus all the things he needed to survive. Patrick's mood grew darker as he soldiered on down the street. He'd go to Westerbridge and see if Freddie was around or perhaps even to the Studios and see if Jane was there. He started to feel better now that he had a plan. Something to do. People to see.

Chapter 18

The waiting was nearly over. David had been accepted at Oxford and now they were waiting to find out if Judy had got into the Art College. Everyone who knew was amazed that David was going to turn down his place if Judy didn't get into the college in Oxford. They pointed out the transport links between places, how easy it would be to travel to see each other, how he'd have a lot of studying to do so perhaps it would be better if he didn't have Judy around. He pointed out in his turn that having Judy around hadn't affected his exam results or Judy's either. They found it easy to study in the same room. But there was another reason why they needed to be in the same place and this revelation came later. None of these well-meaning people need have worried because as Jane Stevens had predicted, Judy was accepted at the college and David went ahead and accepted his place.

Joe suggested to Sandra that they should have a little celebration with friends, particularly those who'd helped, like Richard Jackson, for instance. Sandra had always resisted giving parties, not because she wasn't gregarious but because she was slightly ashamed of where they lived in comparison with the people she met at Rita's. The parties at Regent Square had skewed her view of her own home. She knew she couldn't compete with all that space and splendour in her post-war semi. Just the pleasure of reciprocating hospitality according to your means hadn't occurred to her. Being accepted for who you are simply didn't come into it. It was all about bricks and mortar, décor and furnishings to Sandra. When she was a teenager, dreaming of the future, she'd always presumed that she'd end up somewhere a bit like Regent Square not a semi in a street that looked like a hundred other streets. Deep down she blamed Joe for his liking of a quiet life. He accepted promotions at work but never pushed for them. He was just always grateful for what he got, never demanded his right, as she considered it, to more. She'd been suggesting for a while now that they could afford a bigger, better house. He didn't understand. The house was in a convenient position; they only had one child so they didn't need any more bedrooms, they had a garden and a garage. Why would they need any more or anything different? He liked it. It was a cosy, friendly house and Sandra had a talent for what she liked to call décor.

So when Joe suggested a celebration with a few friends he was taken aback when she agreed and started planning it. It was to be afternoon tea followed later by champagne and cake. They would only invite Tim and Judy, Rita and Edward, Jane and Richard and perhaps Freddie Alexander as he'd been helpful too. Joe was so relieved that Patrick was away because it would have been difficult to explain why he hadn't been invited and even more difficult if he'd just suddenly turned up.

*

Everyone was animated and excited at the successes they were celebrating and chatter and laughter filled the room. It was only after the champagne and toasts to the new students were given that David dropped his bombshell to the small, happy group. First he thanked them for their good wishes and then made his announcement, he and Judy standing in front of them together.

"There's something else to celebrate. We've decided that we'd like to get married before we go to Oxford."

When a couple announce that they're going to get married there's usually a great deal of clapping and congratulations and smiles. But not here. They were stunned.

Joe was the first to break the awful silence.

"You're barely eighteen. Wouldn't it be better to wait until you've finished your courses, got qualified, jobs and whatnot and then you're in a better position to set up home?"

Tim joined in.

"You'll meet a lot of like-minded people at university. Isn't it too early to decide that you've already found the one you want to be with for the rest of your life?"

"Dad", said Judy. "We've known that we want to be together since we very first met. We were five, remember? How much longer do we need?"

Jane in her usual straightforward manner put into words what had crossed everyone's minds.

"Forgive me, but you don't *have* to get married, do you? I do hope you don't mind me spelling it out."

Everyone was secretly grateful that she'd raised the question.

"We thought that's what people might think." David said. "But no, we don't *have* to get married, we just want to, have always wanted to. It's difficult to describe. We went to a talk on reincarnation the other night and we think we must have been together in a previous life because when we first met it was as if we already knew each other and it's been like that ever since. But to get married at our age we'd need our parents' permission so that's why we're telling you now so that in the summer before we go to Oxford we could have the wedding."

Sandra finally made her tongue work although the words had difficulty coming through.

"You can't marry. You're ... you're related."

"Related?" Cried Jane and Richard, and Rita and Edward simultaneously.

Sandra had forgotten that not everyone in the room was privy to the latest news but she didn't care anymore. David must not marry. He'd lost his vocation because of this clinging limpet and now that he knew that his uncle had lost his too, he would think that it was acceptable to behave in this way, ignoring the call from God. Patrick was to blame for that too, she'd decided.

David ignored the cries of "related".

"Cousins can marry."

"Cousins?" The ones not in the know echoed.

They were ignored again as David ploughed on.

"We've looked into it. The Catholic Church doesn't allow it but the Civil Law does. Our country's laws say we can."

"It's called consanguinity and it's against all the laws of nature." Screeched Sandra, he voice now fully working again.

"That only applies to much closer relationships like father and daughter or brother and sister."

Sandra recoiled, beside herself. When David had wanted to be a priest her secret need never have come out or even if he'd wanted to marry anyone but Judy then the secret need not have come out but now that she knew Marie's story she would have to confess. How could she tell her son that the man he knew as his father was not his father? How could she tell her husband that he was not the father of their son? How could she wreck her marriage, her whole life, be hated for evermore? Or should she forever hold her peace as they say before the marriage ceremony? Could she live with that? How could she say to David in front of these people that he and Judy were brother and sister?

Rita stood up.

"I really think this is for the families to discuss and we should go and let you sort this out."

Edward, Jane and Richard and Freddie all agreed and stood up in unison, only too pleased to be going and released from the frenzy. They thanked them awkwardly for the tea and made for the front door. Joe followed them, apologising, but Rita patted his arm, saying that there was nothing to apologise for.

"So if the Catholic Church doesn't allow it, where do you go from there?" Joe asked as he came back into the room.

"It's not banned in the Bible, in fact there are incestuous relationships in the Bible, not that I'm suggesting that the Bible actually promotes it. What I mean is that it's yet one more rule that the Church has decided upon itself. That group of old men who decide how we should all live." David responded.

"But David, as your Mum says, if the Church doesn't allow it, for whatever reason, what are you going to do?" Joe asked gently, feeling that Sandra's mounting hysteria wasn't helpful.

"We'll have to have a civil ceremony in a Register Office."

"But that would be living in sin. The Church wouldn't recognise that as a marriage." Persisted Sandra, wanting them to decide for themselves that they shouldn't marry, desperate not to have to tell the dreadful truth.

"We'll get married in a different church then, Church of England, Temple, Synagogue, Stonehenge - anywhere that doesn't make up its own rules."

David had had enough.

"If we'd said we *had* to get married you wouldn't have waited one minute getting us to the Register Office because of course we wouldn't be able to have an abortion. Why? Because the Church says so." David was shouting now. "It's a never-ending circle. Come on, Judy let's go."

They left and went for a long walk to use up the adrenaline that was streaming through their bodies.

"If they won't give their permission we'll just live together and then see how they'll like that." David muttered. "They'd give their permission if we *had* to get married, as they call it, so perhaps that's what we should do."

"How would I do my Art Course if I was having a baby?"

"You could stuff a pillow up your jumper and just pretend until they gave permission."

They burst out laughing and the horrible day melted away. They dreaded going back home but arranged to meet up, as usual, the next day.

*

Sandra seemed to be waiting for him as he came in.

"David, I must speak to you."

"Oh no, please, I've had enough."

"I'm not going to go over what's already been said. This is something I thought I'd never have to tell you. Please listen."

She seemed distraught.

"Where's Dad?"

"He usually plays chess with Edward on a Friday and he thought it would do him good after all the carry-on. He phoned and Edward was happy for him to go round. That was useful because he must never hear what I've got to say."

David waited.

"You're right that you can marry your cousin, but you can't marry your sister."

David was perplexed.

"What are you saying?"

"Before I married your Dad I was Patrick's girlfriend and very much in love with him."

"But that was years ago. It's got nothing to do with this."

"Please listen and please don't hate me when I tell you."

David looked at his mother who was always his friend and ally when he was a child. Where did it all start going wrong? he asked himself. But he decided to sit down and hear her out although he presumed it was another ploy to stop him marrying.

"After Patrick became a priest he didn't keep in touch much but just once when he had leave he came to stay with us. David, you must believe me when I say that he was a magical person. It was as if he could put a spell on you. I still found him attractive, more than that, I think I was still in love with him. When we were on our own in the house we, we ....."

David remained silent. He didn't offer her the word she was looking for. No doubt she was looking for a euphemism but he could think of words which were more appropriate.

"We made love. When I became pregnant, the conception dated back to that time."

David felt sick at the thought. It repulsed him. But the worst part was that what they had done was going to banish him forever from being with Judy.

"Judy's birthday's only a couple of months after mine. So he had Marie just a short while after you. So he had a vocation did he? Called by God? You wanted him to hand me the chalice?"

He didn't keep the disgust from his voice.

"So weren't you and Dad having sex at that time? You know for definite that Uncle Patrick is my father?"

She cringed. She'd never imagined her own son speaking to her like that.

"Yes, we were. So I never knew which one was the father."

David snatched at the glimmer of hope.

"You mean, Patrick *might* be my father, it's not definite?"

"Yes, but it's too much of a risk. Children born from close relations have deformities. That's why it's banned."

"I'm going to choose from the two options. I'm going to choose that Dad is my Dad. It's 50/50 so I'll take my chance."

"No, David, you mustn't."

"You'll do anything to stop me marrying Judy. You've never liked her. You might even be making this up for all I know. Why have you never liked her?"

"You were always so close that I thought she would eventually take you away from your vocation."

"Mum, I never had a vocation. You were the one who had the vocation."

He went to his room.

*

David and Judy walked to the barn.

"There's no end to what my uncle's done. The whole hideous story just keeps rolling on."

He told Judy the unbearable story his mother had told him.

Judy was sick of the earth suddenly stopping dead in its orbit, sick of the moon being so shocked by earth's standstill that it heaves the oceans out of their beds and hurls them into the sun. She'd had that feeling so many times in the last few years that she wondered how many more times it would happen before the universe really did spin out of control and disintegrate.

David had felt that it was only right that he should tell her but now looking at her beaten expression he couldn't tell what was in her mind. He waited, frightened at what she might say.

"We must remember that it's not definite, it's just a possibility that we're brother and sister. Do you remember when we were kids and your favourite football team was killed? We asked God then to always help us and guide us so that we would always make the right decisions. Let's remind God of that prayer now and ask Him to help us make the right decision."

They stood facing each other with their eyes closed, holding hands. The earth held its breath. They felt the answer at the same moment, opened their eyes and smiled. They'd known the answer even before the prayer.

*

David wrapped her in his arms and whispered his mantra,

"Never will I leave you; never will I forsake you."

Judy whispered back,

"You were mine before we were even born."

A wind blew across their faces as the Earth breathed out a huge sigh.

Perhaps they'd belonged to each other even before the universe was created, waiting in the mind of God.

The End

Printed in Great Britain
by Amazon